The Prison

Georges Simenon

The Prison

Translated from the French by Lyn Moir

A Helen and Kurt Wolff Book
Harcourt, Brace & World, Inc., New York

First edition

Library of Congress Catalog Card Number: 69-12048

Printed in the United States of America

Originally published under the title La Prison

The Prison

Chapter One

How many months, how many years, does it take to turn a child into an adolescent, an adolescent into a man? At what moment can one say that that change has taken place?

There is no solemn proclamation, no giving out of prizes, no diploma, as there is for academic achievements.

Alain Poitaud, at the age of thirty-two, took only a few hours, perhaps only a few minutes, to stop being the man he had been up to that time and to become another.

October 17th. In Paris the rain was falling so heavily and the gusts of wind were so violent that windshield wipers were useless, only making the light from the street lamps more blurred.

Hunched over the steering wheel, he drove slowly along Boulevard de Courcelles, the black railings of Parc Monceau on his right, then turned into Rue de Chazelles, where he lived. It is a short street, lined with apartment houses for the well-to-do. He was lucky to find a parking place for his car almost at his own front door, and he raised his head involuntarily as he slammed the door shut, to see if there was a light on on the top floor.

It had become such a reflex action that he couldn't have

said whether he had done it or not. Besides, he was already plowing through the rain which slapped him in the face and beat on his clothes. He pushed open the door glazed with frosted glass.

A man standing in the doorway as if sheltering from the rain followed him in.

"Monsieur Poitaud?"

The lighting was dim, the walls paneled.

"Yes, that's right," he answered, astonished.

It was an ordinary man, an unprepossessing shape in a dark overcoat. He took a card with a tricolor stripe on it from his pocket.

"Inspector Noble, of the Criminal Police."

Alain looked at him more carefully, curious, but hardly surprised. He was accustomed to meeting all kinds of people.

"May I come up with you for a minute?"

"Have you been waiting for me long?"

"Almost an hour."

"Why didn't you come to see me in my office?"

The detective was young, rather shy, or possibly uneasy. He smiled without answering and the two men went toward the huge elevator—an ancient model with walls covered in crimson velvet.

As the elevator moved slowly upward, they watched each other silently in the soft glow shed by the cut-glass ceiling light. Twice Alain Poitaud opened his mouth to ask a question, but he decided to wait until he was in his own apartment.

The elevator stopped at the third floor, the top floor. Alain turned the key in the lock and pushed the door open. He was surprised to find the apartment in darkness.

"My wife isn't home yet," he remarked mechanically as he reached out for the light switch.

Water was dripping from their overcoats onto the pale blue carpet.

"Take your coat off."

"It's hardly worth while."

Alain looked at him, surprised. His visitor had waited for an hour, barely sheltered by the doorway, and he already knew that his visit was to be so short that he wouldn't take off his wet coat.

Alain pushed open a double swinging door, reached out for some other switches, and several lights lit up an enormous room, one complete wall of which was window, battered by the rain sliding down the glass in thick streams.

"My wife should be here."

He looked at his watch even though there was an antique clock standing in front of him, its bronze pendulum swinging back and forth, ticking softly with each movement.

It was a quarter to eight.

"We're having dinner with some friends soon, and . . ."

He was talking to himself. His idea had been to undress quickly, take a shower, and put on a dark suit.

"Won't you sit down?"

He wasn't worried or upset. Well, hardly. Just a little annoyed by this unexpected person who was keeping him from doing what he had to do. Surprised, too, that Jacqueline was not there.

"Have you a gun, Monsieur Poitaud?"

"Do you mean a pistol?"

"Yes, that's what I had in mind."

"Yes, there's one in the drawer of my bedside table."

"Would you show it to me?"

The inspector spoke softly, hesitantly. Alain went toward a door, the bedroom door, and his companion followed him.

The walls of the room were covered with yellow silk, the gigantic bed with wildcat fur. The furniture was lacquered white.

Alain opened a drawer, looked surprised, pushed his hand in to the back of the drawer, among the odds and ends.

"It's not there," he murmured.

Then he looked all around as if to remember where he could have put the weapon.

The two top drawers of the chest of drawers were his, the lower drawers belonged to Jacqueline. Nobody called her Jacqueline. To him, as to everyone else, she was Kitten, a nickname he had given her several years before, because she looked like a little cat.

Handkerchiefs, shirts, underwear . . .

"When did you see it last?"

"This morning, probably. . . ."

"Aren't you sure?"

This time he turned to face his companion and looked at him, frowning.

"Listen, Inspector . . . For five years, ever since we have lived here, that pistol has been in the drawer of the bedside table. . . . Every evening, when I undress, I use that drawer to put everything in my pockets in. . . . I put my keys there, my wallet, my cigarette case, my lighter, my checkbook, my change. . . . I'm so used to seeing the pistol in there where it belongs that I no longer notice it. . . ."

"Wouldn't you have noticed its not being there?"

He thought for a moment.

"I don't think so. It must have slid to the back of the drawer several times. . . ."

"When did you see your wife last?"

"Has something happened to her?"

"Not in the way you think. Did you have lunch with her?"

"No. I was at the printer's for page make-up and I had sandwiches at the imposing stone."

"Did she telephone you at all during the day?"

"No."

He had to think, for Kitten often telephoned him.

"Didn't you call her, either?"

"She isn't often here during the day. She has a job, you see. She is a journalist and . . . But tell me what the point of these questions is."

"I'd rather my chief told you. Will you come with me to the Quai des Orfèvres, where they'll tell you all about it?"

"Are you sure that my wife . . ."

"She isn't dead, or injured."

Politely, shyly, the inspector went toward the door and Alain followed him, too dazed to think.

Without a word being said on either part, they did not ring for the elevator, so majestic and slow, but walked down the thickly carpeted stair. The windows on each landing were of stained glass in the style of 1900.

"I imagine your wife has her own car?"

"Yes. A very small one, the same as the one I drive in Paris, the one at the door. More of a mini."

At the doorstep they both hesitated.

"How did you get here?"

"By métro."

"You won't feel embarrassed if I drive you?"

He was managing to hang on to a good part of his irony. He was ironic by nature, sometimes rather aggressively so. Wasn't that the only reasonable attitude toward the stupidity of life and of other people?

"I'm sorry. There's hardly enough room for your legs."

He drove quickly. His tiny English car was fast, and he shot through a red light.

"I'm sorry. . . ."

"It doesn't matter. I have nothing to do with traffic offenses."

"Shall I drive into the courtyard?"

"Yes, please."

The inspector leaned through the car window to say something to the two men at the gate.

"Is my wife here?"

"Very likely."

What good was there in questioning this man who wouldn't tell him anything? In a few minutes he would find himself face to face with a superintendent, almost certainly a superintendent he knew, for he had met almost all of them.

He started up the main staircase of his own accord and stopped at the first floor.

"Is this the place?"

The long, badly lit corridor was empty, and the doors on both sides were all closed. There was only the elderly usher, a silver chain around his neck, a heavy medal on his chest, standing in front of a table covered with green cloth, like a billiard table.

"Would you go into the waiting room for a moment?"

One wall was all windows, like the artist's studio that they had made their living room, and there was no one there but an old woman dressed in black who watched him come in, her small eyes black and beady.

"Excuse me . . ."

The inspector went into the corridor and knocked at a door that he closed behind him. He did not emerge again from the room he had entered. No one came. The old woman didn't move. Even the air around them was still and gray, like fog.

He looked at his watch again. Twenty past eight. It was hardly an hour since he had left his office in Rue de Marignan, after calling to Maleski:

"See you shortly. . . ."

They were going to have dinner together, along with a dozen or so friends, men and women, in a new restaurant on Avenue de Suffren.

In this place the rain and the storm had no existence. One was suspended in time and space. On any other day Alain would only have had to write his name on a slip of paper and a few minutes later the usher would have shown him into the office of the head of the Criminal Police, who would have shaken hands with him.

It was a long time since he had had to wait in a waiting room. It had only happened to him at the beginning of his career.

He glanced at the old woman. Her lack of movement impressed him, made him wonder how long she had been there. For hours, maybe?

He grew impatient and began to feel stifled. He got up, lit a cigarette, and began to walk up and down while the woman looked at him reproachfully.

After that he opened the glass door, strode along the

corridor, and planted himself in front of the man with the silver chain.

"Which superintendent wants to see me?"

"I don't know, sir."

"There can't be many of them still in their offices at this time of night."

"Two or three. Those fellows sometimes stay very late. What is your name?"

"Alain Poitaud."

"You're a married man, aren't you?"

"Yes, I'm married."

"Your wife is small and dark, and she's wearing a fur-lined raincoat?"

"That's quite right."

"In that case, it's Deputy Superintendent Roumagne."

"Is my wife in his office?"

"I don't know, sir."

"Have you seen her?"

"I certainly have seen her."

"Did she come here alone?"

"You must excuse me, but I have already said too much."

Alain began to walk again, almost as humiliated as he was upset. He was being made to wait. He was being treated like an ordinary person. What could Kitten have come to the Quai des Orfèvres to do? What was all this about a pistol?

Why was it no longer in its place in the drawer? It was an ordinary sort of pistol, one that any burglar would have laughed at, a little 6.35 made at Herstal. He hadn't bought it. One of his colleagues, Bob Demarie, had given it to him.

"Now that my son's really walking about, I'd rather not have a thing like that lying around the apartment."

That had been at least four or five years ago. Since then, Demarie had had two other children.

What could Kitten . . .

"Monsieur Poitaud!"

It was his inspector, at the other end of the corridor. He was signaling him to come. Alain strode forward.

"In here, please. . . ."

There was no one in the deputy superintendent's office except the deputy superintendent himself, a man of about forty who looked tired. He shook hands with Alain before sitting down again.

"Take your coat off. Sit down, Monsieur Poitaud."

The inspector had not followed him in.

"I'm told that your pistol has disappeared."

"I couldn't find it in its usual place."

"Could this be it?"

He held out a black, or rather bluish, Browning. Poitaud took hold of it automatically.

"I suppose so. It could be."

"Did yours have any distinguishing marks?"

"To tell you the truth, I've never looked at it carefully. I've never used it, either, not even in the country, to try it out."

"Your wife knew about it, of course?"

"Of course."

He found himself suddenly wondering if it was really he sitting there, humbly answering silly questions. He was Alain Poitaud, damn it. Everyone in Paris knew him. He was the head of one of the biggest weekly magazines in France, and he was getting ready to launch another. Besides, for the last six months he had been making records that were talked about daily on the radio.

Not only did he not wait in waiting rooms, there were at

least four Ministers whom he called *tu* and at whose house he dined, when it wasn't they who put themselves out to come to dinner with him at his country house.

He had to struggle, to wrench himself out of this kind of stupid sense of unreality.

"Would you kindly tell me what all this is getting at?"

The superintendent gave him a bored, tired look.

"I'm just coming to that, Monsieur Poitaud. Don't think I'm enjoying this any more than you are. I've had a very hard day. I was in a hurry to get home, to be with my wife and children."

He looked at the black marble clock on the mantelpiece.

"You've been married for quite a while, haven't you?"

"It must be six years now. No, seven. Not counting the two years when we were as good as married."

"You have a child."

"A son."

The policeman looked down at his file.

"He is five years old."

"That's quite correct."

"He doesn't live with you."

"That's not quite so correct."

"What do you mean by that?"

"We have an apartment, a *pied-à-terre* really, in Paris, because we go out a lot in the evenings. On Friday afternoons we go back to our real home, at Saint-Illiers-la-Ville, in the Forest of Rosny. In the summer we spend almost every night there."

"I see. Naturally, you love your wife."

"Naturally."

He did not say it with passion, or with heat, but as if that went without saying.

"You know all about her private life?"

"Her private life is spent with me. As for her professional life . . ."

"That's what I meant."

"My wife is a journalist."

"Doesn't she work for your magazine?"

"No. That would be too easy. Anyway, it isn't her type of work."

"How does she get on with her sister?"

"With Adrienne? Very well. They came to Paris one after the other, Kitten first. . . ."

"Kitten?"

"It's an affectionate nickname I gave my wife. My friends and my colleagues have come to call her that too. When she was looking for a name to sign her articles with, I suggested Jacqueline Kitten. She and her sister shared a room in Saint-Germain-des-Prés for a long time."

"Did you meet them both at the same time?"

"The first time?"

"Yes."

"No. Kitten was by herself."

"Didn't she introduce her sister to you?"

"Later on. Several months later. If you know all this, why are you asking me these questions? It's about time you told me what has happened to my wife."

"Nothing has happened to your wife."

He said that in a sad, dull voice.

"To whom, then?"

"To your sister-in-law."

"An accident?"

While he was asking this question, his glance fell on the automatic lying on the desk.

"She's been . . ."

"Murdered, yes."

Alain didn't have the courage to ask who had killed her. He had never before known that feeling of stupor, of inner emptiness. His brain wasn't working, or at least not as well as it usually did. He felt himself caught up in a world that had become incoherent, where words no longer had the same meaning, or objects the same appearance.

"She was killed this afternoon, a little before five o'clock, by your wife."

"That's ridiculous."

"It's true, though."

"Who gave you that idea?"

"Your wife. And also the nurse who was in the apartment at the time."

"What about my brother-in-law?"

"He is making his statement in the office next door."

"Where is my wife?"

"Upstairs, with the Criminal Identity boys."

"But why? Did she tell you why?"

He blushed suddenly and turned away from the deputy superintendent's look.

"I was hoping that you would tell me that."

He wasn't sad, or overcome, or moved. He wasn't angry either. It was more a feeling of loss of identity, and he might well have pinched himself to make sure that it was really he, Alain Poitaud, who was sitting there, on the edge of a green armchair, facing a mahogany desk dominated by the tired face of the superintendent. How could it be a question of Kitten, and of Adrienne with her neat, sweet features, her big blue eyes with their long lashes?

"I don't understand," he confessed, shaking his head as if to wake himself up.

"What don't you understand?"

"That my wife could have shot her sister. You did say that Adrienne was dead, didn't you?"

"Almost at once."

The word "almost" jarred on him and he stared at the Browning on the desk. That meant that she had been alive, for a few minutes or a few seconds, after the shot. And what about Kitten, during that time? What was she doing, gun in hand? Was she watching her sister dying? Did she try to get help for her?

"Didn't she try to run away?"

"No. We found her in the apartment, standing with her face pressed against the window."

The window with cold rain running down it.

"What did she say?"

"She sighed and murmured: 'At last!' "

"What about Bobo?"

"Who is Bobo?"

"My sister-in-law's little boy. She has two children, a boy and a girl."

The girl, who looked so much like her mother, was called Nelle.

"The nurse took them into the kitchen and a maid kept them there while the nurse tried to do something for the dying woman."

There was something wrong there. The superintendent had said at first that she had died almost at once. Now he was talking about the nurse doing something for the dying woman. He knew the apartment on Rue de l'Université, on the first floor of an old private mansion, with tall windows and a ceiling that was known to have been painted by one of Poussin's pupils.

"Tell me, Monsieur Poitaud, what were your relations with your sister-in-law?"

"They were good."

"What I want you to tell me is exactly what those relations were."

"What difference would that make?"

"We aren't dealing with a murder for profit, are we? There weren't any money troubles between the two women, were there?"

"Certainly not."

"I don't suppose that it's a question of one of those old feuds you get in some families, either, is it?"

"No."

"Bear in mind the fact that juries are hardly ever severe in the case of a *crime passionnel.*"

They looked at each other. The superintendent, whose name Alain had already forgotten, was playing the game with no thought for finesse and was asking the questions with obvious boredom.

"Were you her lover?"

"No. Yes. I mean that can't be the reason. It was too long ago. Do you understand?"

He was following a train of thought, realizing all the time that his spoken words were dragging far behind. He would have needed a lot of time to go into details, to explain that . . .

"It's at least a year since . . . No, not quite . . . Not since last Christmas . . ."

"That this affair began?"

"On the contrary, that it ended."

"Completely?"

"Yes."

"Were you the one to break it off?"

He shook his head. He wanted to hide his head in his hands. For the first time he realized the difficulty, if not the impossibility, of explaining what had really happened.

"It wasn't a really intimate relationship. . . ."

"What do you mean?"

"I don't know. . . . It began . . ."

"Tell me how it began, then."

"It was stupid. . . . Kitten and I weren't yet married, but we were already living together. . . ."

"How long ago was that?"

"Eight years, maybe? I hadn't started up the magazine and I was earning my living by writing newspaper articles. . . . I was writing songs, too. . . . We lived in a hotel in Saint-Germain-des-Prés. . . . Kitten was working too. . . ."

"Wasn't she a student at one time?"

He had glanced at his file again to refresh his memory, and Alain wondered what else there could be in that file.

"Yes. She studied philosophy for two years."

"Go on."

"One day . . ."

It had been raining, as it was today. He had come home toward the end of the afternoon and had found not his wife but Adrienne in the room.

"Jacqueline won't be in for dinner. She's busy interviewing an American author at the Hôtel George V."

"What are you doing here?"

"Nothing. I came by to see her for a minute. She had to go and so I said to myself that I'd wait for you."

At that time she wasn't quite twenty. In appearance she was as calm and passive as Kitten was demonstrative.

The superintendent was waiting somewhat impatiently. He lit a cigarette and held the pack out to Alain, who lit one too.

"It happened so naturally that I'd find it difficult to tell how it did happen."

"Did she love you?"

"Maybe. Two years ago I would probably have said yes. Now, I wouldn't like to say. . . ."

Everything had become so different since the timid, polite inspector had followed him through the doorway of the apartment house and had asked if he might go upstairs with him.

"I think all sisters . . . I shouldn't say all, but many of them . . . I know personally of several cases among my circle of friends . . ."

"Your affair lasted for about seven years, then?"

"It wasn't an affair. . . . I must explain that to you. . . . We never made each other any declarations of undying love. . . . I went on loving Kitten and I married her a few months later."

"Why?"

"Why did I marry her? But . . ."

There was that point, why had he? The truth was that on the night he had asked her to marry him he was drunk.

"You were living together. . . . You didn't have any children. . . ."

At a table in some bar, surrounded by friends who were as tight as he was, he had announced:

"We're getting married in three weeks, Kitten and I."

"Why three weeks?"

"The time for publishing the banns."

There had been an argument, some claiming that the banns had to be read for two weeks, others agreeing that it was three.

"We'll soon see, won't we? What do you think about it, Kitten?"

She had snuggled close to him without answering.

"So after you were married you went on seeing your sister-in-law."

"With my wife, usually."

"And elsewhere?"

"From time to time. There was a time when we saw each other once a week. . . ."

"Where?"

"At her place. . . . In the room that she'd had to herself since her sister had left it."

"Was she working?"

"She was taking some classes in art history."

"And after she married?"

"She was away for a month with her husband. When she got back, she called me up and arranged a meeting. I took her to a furnished room in Rue de Longchamp."

"Didn't your brother-in-law suspect anything?"

"Certainly not."

He was flabbergasted at being asked such a question. Roland Blanchet was much too much the Superintendent of Finances and too sure of himself to imagine for one moment that his wife could have anything to do with another man.

"I presume you haven't asked him that question?"

"One murder's enough, isn't it?" the policeman said dryly. "What about your wife?"

"She didn't either. She thought we were good friends. . . . At the very beginning, before her sister got married, she said one time:

" 'It's a pity a man can't have two wives.'

"I took that to mean that she was thinking of Adrienne. . . ."

"And after that? Didn't her opinions change?"

"How can I answer that, after what I've just learned? Adrienne and I happened not to see each other for two or three months. . . . She has two children. . . . We, for our part, have one. . . . Their country house is on the other side of Paris from ours, in the Forest of Orléans. . . ."

"What happened at Christmas?"

"It was the day before Christmas Eve. . . . We saw each other . . ."

"In the furnished room as usual?"

"Yes. . . . We remained faithful to it. . . . Since we were each going to spend the holiday with our own families, we had decided to share a bottle of champagne, before meeting again in January."

"Who decided to break it off?"

He had to think.

"I suppose she did. . . . It had become a habit—do you understand? I was getting busier and busier. . . . She said something like:

" 'Your heart's not in it any more, is it, Alain?' "

"Did you want to finish with the affair, too?"

"Perhaps. . . . You're asking me questions I've never asked myself. . . ."

"Get it into your head that two hours ago I had never heard of your wife, or your sister-in-law, and if I knew your name it was only because of your magazine. . . ."

"I'm doing my best to answer. . . ."

He seemed to be apologizing, which was not in character for him. Nothing he had done since entering the Criminal Police building was in character.

"I remember that I suggested making love one last time."

"Did she agree to that?"

"She preferred to have us part just as good friends. . . ."

"And then?"

"Then nothing. Kitten and I used to go to dinner at her house. . . . We used to meet her and her husband at the theater or in a restaurant. . . ."

"Has your wife changed in any way?"

He tried hard to remember the slightest indication of change, and shook his head.

"No. . . . I don't know. . . . I'm sorry I'm repeating those words so often, but that's all I can say. . . ."

"Did you have dinner together every evening?"

"Almost every evening."

"Alone together?"

"Very rarely. . . . We have a lot of friends, and we have to go to a lot of cocktail parties and dinners. . . ."

"And on weekends?"

"On Saturdays we have a quiet day, but Kitten almost always has an article to write. . . . She sometimes has to stay in Paris longer than I do. . . . She specializes in interviewing personalities who are passing through the city. . . . But let's come to the point—tell me, why would she have killed her sister?"

He was rebelling, shocked at seeing himself lay bare his marital life and his love life before a tired policeman.

"That's what we're trying to get at, both of us, aren't we?"

"It's not possible . . ."

"What's not possible?"

"That she could suddenly have become so jealous of Adrienne that . . ."

"Were you very much in love, you and your wife?"

"I've told you so."

"You've told me about the beginning, in Saint-Germain-des-Prés. . . . But after that?"

"We love each other, yes."

Wasn't the proof of that the fact that he was so shattered that he couldn't get his bearings? Half an hour or an hour before, Kitten must have been sitting in the chair he was in now, the same light with its glass shade lighting her face.

"Did you ask *her* that?"

"She refused to answer my questions."

"So she hasn't confessed, then?"

He had a momentary ray of hope.

"She has confessed to shooting her sister, that's all."

"Hasn't she explained why?"

"No. I told her she should call in a lawyer, one of her own choosing."

"What did she say to that?"

"That that was your affair and that, as far as she was concerned, she couldn't care less."

The "couldn't care less" wasn't Kitten. That didn't sound like her choice of words. She must have used another phrase.

"How was she?"

"She seemed calm. It was she who looked at her watch and said to me:

" 'Alain and I should be meeting in the apartment at half past seven. He'll be worried.' "

"Did she seem upset?"

"To tell the truth, no, she didn't. I've seen, here in this office, many men and women who have just committed a crime. I don't remember ever seeing anyone show such self-control or such indifference."

"That's because you don't know Kitten. . . ."

"If I've got it right, you haven't often been together, just the two of you. I mean these last few years."

"Together, yes. Alone together, no. You mustn't forget my job, which obliges me to see people all day and often into the small hours. . . ."

"Do you have a mistress, Monsieur Poitaud?"

That word again! It didn't mean anything, and seemed so old-fashioned to him.

"If you are asking if I sleep with women other than my wife, I'll answer right away that I do. . . . Not with one, but with dozens. . . . Every time I have the chance and it seems worth while. . . ."

"Given the character of your magazine, you must have a good many chances."

There was a trace of envy in the superintendent's voice.

"So, to recap—you know nothing. You have had an affair with your sister-in-law, an affair that ended in December last year and, as far as you know, your wife knew nothing about it. We still have to get to the root of the matter, to understand why."

Alain looked at him curiously, shocked. What could this man, this man who knew nothing of their life, hope to understand, since he himself didn't understand a thing?

"What paper did your wife work for, in fact?"

"For none of them and for all of them. . . . She was what we call a free-lance—that is, she worked for herself. . . .

When she had written an article, or a series of articles, she knew what paper to offer it to. . . . She did a lot of work for English and American magazines. . . ."

"Not for yours?"

"You've asked me that already. No. It's not her sort of thing."

"Have you a lawyer, Monsieur Poitaud?"

"Of course."

"Would you ask him to get in touch with me this evening or tomorrow morning?"

The superintendent got up with a sigh of relief.

"I'm going to ask you to go next door. You will repeat the main points of your statement and a stenographer will take it all down."

Just like Blanchet a little earlier. What could Blanchet have told them? How had he, with his eminent position in the Bank of France, how had he taken the humiliation of being questioned by a police officer?

The superintendent had opened the door.

"I'm sorry I kept you so long, Monsieur Poitaud. I'll see you tomorrow."

"When may I see my wife?"

"That's up to the magistrate to decide."

"Where will she be spending the night?"

"Down there, at the Central Police Station."

"Don't I need to take her anything, underwear, toilet things . . . ?"

"If you want. Usually, the first night . . ."

He didn't finish the sentence.

"You only need to leave a suitcase at Quai de l'Horloge."

"I know where."

The cells, the courtyard, the room where a doctor examined the women . . . He had written an article about it ten years previously.

"I'll phone you when I need you."

The deputy superintendent put on his hat and coat.

"Perhaps you'll have had some ideas by then," and, opening a door: "Good night, Julien."

The office was smaller than the one they had just left, with deal furniture instead of mahogany.

"Your surname, Christian name, age, profession . . ."

"Alain Poitaud, born in Paris, on Place Clichy, age thirty-two, head of *Toi* magazine. . . ."

"Married?"

"Yes, married. With one child. Address in Paris: 17 bis Rue de Chazelles. Address of permanent residence: Les Nonnettes, Saint-Illiers-la-Ville. . . ."

"You declare . . ."

"I'm not declaring anything. An inspector came up to my apartment with me and asked me if I owned a gun. . . . I said I did and I looked for my Browning in the drawer where it usually is. . . . It wasn't there any longer. . . . The inspector brought me here and a superintendent whose name I've forgotten . . ."

"Deputy Superintendent Roumagne."

"That's it. This Superintendent Roumagne, then, told me that my wife had killed her sister. . . . He showed me a Browning which I think I recognize as mine, although it hasn't any distinguishing marks and I've never used it. . . . He asked me if I knew any reason for my wife's action, and I told him that I can't think of one. . . ."

He walked back and forth as if he were in his own office, smoking his cigarette nervously.

"Is that all?"

"There was another matter, but I don't suppose it should appear in the report."

"What was it about?"

"My relationship with my sister-in-law . . ."

"An intimate one?"

"It was . . ."

"Some time ago?"

"It's been over for a year . . ."

Julien scratched his forehead with his pencil.

"There'll be time to add that tomorrow if the superintendent thinks it's relevant."

"May I go now?"

"Yes, as far as I'm concerned, and since you've finished next door. . . ."

The long corridor felt damp to him. The old woman wasn't in the glass-paneled waiting room any more, and another usher was wearing the silver chain and the medal. Downstairs, he found it was still raining, with some short, heavy, squally gusts as well, but he didn't demean himself by running to his car, and he was soaked when he got into it.

Chapter Two

STILL having to hunch forward to see through all the rain on the windshield, he drove up Champs-Elysées again, not even trying to put his ideas in order. He was annoyed with the shy policeman, with Superintendent Roumagne, with Julien, the indifferent stenographer, for having humiliated him, or, more correctly, for having confused him so much with their questions that he didn't know where he stood.

Seeing an empty parking place in front of a bar, he stopped abruptly, just missing being hit by the car behind him. The driver shook his fist at him and swore. He needed a drink. He didn't know the bar, and the bartender didn't know him either.

"A scotch . . . double. . . ."

He drank a lot. Kitten did too. And so, for the most part, did all their friends and acquaintances. He, at least, was lucky in that he never got really drunk nor did he have a hangover the next morning.

It was unthinkable that his wife, after a year . . .

He almost made a half turn to speak to her, as if she were sitting on the next stool. That was where she usually was.

What precisely had the deputy superintendent wanted to

know about their relationship? How could he have explained it? He had been asked if they still loved each other. What did the word "love" mean?

It wasn't the kind of relationship the policeman seemed to imagine. He would be in his office in Rue de Marignan, or at the printer's. She would phone him:

"Have you any plans for this evening?"

He didn't ask her where she was. She didn't ask him what he was doing.

"Not yet."

"Where shall I meet you?"

"Say eight o'clock, at the Clocheton."

That was a bar opposite his office building. There were a few bars like that in Paris where they used to meet. She would sometimes wait an hour for him without getting impatient. He would sit down beside her.

"A double scotch."

They wouldn't kiss or ask each other any questions, except:

"Where are we having dinner?"

It would almost always be in a bistrot that was more or less in fashion. If they went there alone they would find friends already there, and they would end up by making up a table of eight or ten.

She always sat beside him. He wouldn't pay any special attention to her, he would only have a feeling that she was there, at his side. She wouldn't keep him from drinking or, later on in the evening, from inventing silly games, like getting in front of a fast-moving car to test the driver's reflexes. He had just escaped being killed a hundred times. His friends too.

"Let's go and break things up at Hortense's!"

That was a night club they often went to. Hortense was fond of them, though at the same time she was a bit afraid of them.

"It's a bit dull in here, old girl. Who's that old fool sitting opposite me?"

"Be quiet, Alain. It's an important man who . . ."

"I don't like his tie."

Hortense would resign herself to the inevitable. Alain would get up, go over to the man opposite, and greet him cheerfully.

"I don't like your tie, you know. No, I don't like it at all."

The man, accompanied by a woman more often than not, wouldn't know what to say.

"With your kind permission."

With a swift movement he would wrench it off the other, take a pair of scissors out of his pocket, and begin to cut it up.

"You can keep this bit as a souvenir."

Some of them didn't turn a hair. Others, getting angry, would almost always end up beating a retreat.

He emptied his glass in one gulp, licked his lips, and paid for the drink. Once again he pushed through the curtain of rain and shut himself in his car.

When he got home he put all the lights on, wondering, meanwhile, what he was going to do. It was an odd feeling to be there without Kitten.

He should have been on Avenue de Suffren at that moment, in the new restaurant Peter had found, where a dozen of them had been going to have dinner together. Should he phone them and say he wasn't coming?

He shrugged his shoulders and went toward the fitted bar in one corner of the studio-living room. A famous painter had worked there once, a portrait painter whose name everyone had forgotten. That had been around 1910.

He didn't like to drink by himself.

"Your health, my dear!"

He held his glass up, leaning toward an imaginary Kitten. Then he stared at the telephone.

Whom should he call? He felt there was someone he ought to call, but he no longer remembered who. He had had nothing to eat, but that didn't matter. He wasn't hungry.

If only he had one close friend . . .

He had plenty of pals, dozens of pals, men who worked with him on the magazine, actors, producers, singers, not counting bartenders and *maîtres d'hôtel.*

"Listen, chum . . ."

He always called everyone "chum." Adrienne too. Ever since the day he'd met her. He hadn't been the one to start the affair. He had thought her too calm, too colorless, for his taste. He had been wrong in that. She was not colorless; it had taken him months to realize that.

What would her idiot of a husband be thinking? Alain didn't like Blanchet. He detested people of that sort, so sure of themselves, so dignified and starchy, without the slightest trace of imagination.

What if he were to telephone Blanchet? Only to find out how he had taken the news. . . .

His glance fell on the chest of drawers, and he remembered that he ought to take some underwear and toilet articles to his wife. Their suitcases were in the closets in the hallway. He chose one of an appropriate size.

What on earth does a woman in a cell at the Central Police Station wear? The drawer was full of sheer lingerie, and he was surprised to find she had so much. He chose some nylon blouses, some panties, and three pairs of pajamas. Then he made sure that there was a toothbrush and soap in the crocodile-leather toilet bag.

He wondered whether to have another drink, then shrugged his shoulders and went out, locking the door behind him and leaving the lights on. He drove across a good part of the city through the rain, which had become a little less heavy. Now it was an autumn rain, soft, slow, and cold, which looked as if it were going to last for several days. People on foot were walking quickly, leaning over, leaping to one side as cars passed, splashing them as they went.

Quai de l'Horloge. A dim light over the stone doorway. A corridor, very wide, very long, like a subway. At the far end of this a uniformed policeman was sitting behind a desk. The policeman watched him approaching with the suitcase and seemed a little curious.

"You do have a Madame Jacqueline Poitaud here, don't you?"

"Just a minute."

He looked at his register.

"That's right."

"Would you see that she gets this suitcase?"

"I'll have to consult my chief."

He went over and knocked at a door, disappeared through it, and came back a few minutes later with a fat man with his tie loosened, his shirt collar unbuttoned, and the belt of his trousers unbuckled.

"You're the husband, are you?"

"Yes."

"Let's see your papers."

He held them out and the man looked at them for a long time.

"So you're the man who does that magazine with the odd pictures? I'll have to check what's in this suitcase."

"Open it, then."

"According to the rules, you're the one who should open it."

It was as if the three of them were in a badly lit tunnel. Alain opened the suitcase and then the toilet bag. The officer ran his fingers through the underwear and removed the nail scissors, nail file, and tweezers from the toilet bag, leaving only the toothbrush and soap.

He handed the forbidden objects one by one to Alain, who stuffed them mechanically into his pocket.

"Will you take it to her now?"

The man checked the time on a big pocket watch.

"It's half past ten. According to the rules . . ."

"How is she?"

"I haven't seen her."

Of course, not everyone was interested in what Kitten was doing.

"Has she a cell to herself?"

"Certainly not. We're overcrowded just now."

"You don't know who's in with her?"

The other man shrugged his shoulders.

"Prostitutes, probably. They keep bringing them in to us. Look! Another batch coming in."

A Black Maria had stopped at the edge of the sidewalk, and plain-clothes policemen were pushing a group of women through the doorway. Alain passed them as he went out. Some of them smiled at him. He could see that most of them were regulars, but there were three or four young girls with worried expressions in their eyes.

What was he going to do? He never went home so early in

the evening, even when Kitten was there. Unless he drank himself into a stupor he wouldn't sleep, and he had no desire to think the things that were crowding into his head.

In twenty, in fifty bars or night clubs he would be sure to find people he had called "chum" for years, people who, after shaking hands with him, would say:

"Scotch?"

Women too, women of all kinds, those he had slept with and those with whom he hadn't yet or with whom he had no desire to.

The seat beside him was cold and empty.

Should he go to Rue de l'Université? To his brother-in-law's?

What kind of expression could his dignified and self-important brother-in-law have shown when he learned that his wife had just been killed by a bullet in . . .

In fact, no one had told Alain whether Kitten had aimed at the head or the heart. The one thing he knew was that afterward she had pressed her face to the window, a gesture that was, indeed, very characteristic of her. She often did that. When he was speaking to her she wouldn't move and, a long time later, she would turn around and ask, innocently:

"Did you say something?"

"What were you thinking about?"

"Nothing. You know perfectly well I never think about anything. . . ."

She was a strange girl. So was Adrienne, with her huge long-lashed eyes completely lacking in expression most of the time. All girls were odd. Men too. One talks about them without knowing a thing about them. One writes things about them, both women and men, that haven't the slightest connection with the truth. Wasn't he himself an odd man, too?

A policeman who had just come out into the street and was buckling his belt on took a couple of steps forward to look at him. Alain decided to drive off.

Tomorrow morning the newspapers . . . He was amazed that he hadn't met any reporters and photographers yet. The police must be trying to keep the case quiet as long as possible. Would that be out of consideration for him or for his brother-in-law, who held an important public office?

All the Blanchets held important public offices, the father and the three sons. When the first son was born they must have decided:

"The Polytechnique for him!"

For the second, the Ecole Normale Supérieur. For the third, the Inspection des Finances.

It had worked out, too. They were all important men, all settled in enormous offices complete with an usher wearing a chain of office at the door.

They stank!

"Hell! Hell! And again hell!"

He had had enough. He wanted to do something, to speak to someone, but he still didn't know who. He stopped in Rue de Rivoli and went into a bar he knew.

"Hello, Gaston."

"Are you alone, Monsieur Alain?"

"It can happen to anyone."

"A double scotch?"

He shrugged his shoulders. Why should he suddenly change his habits?

"I hope Madame Kitten is well?"

"Very well, I imagine."

"Isn't she in Paris?"

Once again he felt the need to shock someone.

"She's in Paris all right. In the very center, what you might call the heart of Paris."

Gaston looked at him uncomprehendingly. A couple at the bar, listening, looked at him in the mirror behind the bottles.

"My wife is at the Central."

The word didn't seem to mean anything to the bartender.

"Don't you know the Central Police Station, on Quai de l'Horloge?"

The other man tried to smile, for no reason in particular.

"She killed her sister."

"Was it an accident?"

"That's hardly likely, since she was holding a gun."

"You're joking, aren't you?"

"You'll read all about it in the papers tomorrow morning. Keep the change."

He put a hundred-franc note on the bar, got down from the stool without having decided anything, and a quarter of an hour later found himself in his own street. On the sidewalk by his entrance there was a group of at least twenty people. It was easy to recognize the photographers among them by their gear.

"Got a moment for us, Alain?"

"Get on with it then, boys. . . ."

He posed by the open door of the car, standing at the edge of the sidewalk, and then again lighting a cigarette. The reporters had their notebooks ready.

"Tell me, Monsieur Poitaud . . ."

That was a young chap who didn't yet know that everybody called him Alain.

"Don't you think it's a bit wet out here, boys? Why don't you come up to the apartment?"

One would have had to know him very well, as well as Kitten did, to notice that his voice didn't sound natural. It wasn't a dull voice, although on Quai des Orfèvres it had sounded dull. On the contrary, it had a metallic ring.

"Come on in, since you're here . . ."

Eight of them piled into the elevator while the others ran up the stairs. They all met up in the hall and Alain searched for his key, which he eventually found in a pocket where he didn't usually put it.

"Thirsty?" he asked, throwing his coat over a chair as he went toward the bar.

The photographers hesitated, then decided to get down to work. Alain didn't bat an eyelid while the cameras clicked.

"Whisky for everyone?"

Only one man asked for fruit juice. Their wet feet made dull marks on the pale blue carpet. A tall, bony man, his raincoat soaked through, was sitting on an armchair upholstered in white satin.

The telephone rang. Alain walked slowly over to the instrument. He was holding his glass in the other hand and drank half the contents before speaking.

"Yes, this is Alain. . . . Of course I'm at home, since I'm talking to you. . . . Of course I recognize your voice. . . . I hope you're not shocked that I'm still calling you *tu*, are you? . . ."

He turned to the newspapermen and explained:

"It's my brother-in-law. . . . The husband. . . ."

Then, into the telephone:

"You came here? . . . When? . . . You just missed me. . . . I went to take some clothes to Kitten. . . . We must just have missed each other at the Criminal Police. . . . You were in one office and I was in the one next door. . . .

"What's that? . . . You think I'm playing the fool? . . . I'm sorry to tell you this again at such a time, but you are a pompous idiot and you always will be. . . . I'm just as upset as you are, if not more so. . . . That's not the word for it. . . . Shattered. . . .

"What? . . . What did they ask me? . . . What I knew about it, of course. . . . I told them I didn't know anything at all. . . . It's the truth. . . . Do *you* know anything? . . . Have you any ideas?"

The reporters were taking notes swiftly, the photographers clicking away. The smell of whisky began to fill the studio.

"Help yourselves, chums. . . ."

"What's that you're saying?" His brother-in-law grew worried. "Aren't you alone?"

"There are—wait a minute while I count them—there are nineteen people here including me. . . . Don't worry, it's not an orgy. . . . Eight photographers. . . . The rest are reporters. . . . A young lady has just come in, she's a journalist, too. . . . Help yourself to a drink, chum. . . ."

"How long are they going to stay in your apartment?"

"Do you want me to ask them? How long do you expect to stay here, boys?"

Then, into the mouthpiece:

"About half an hour. . . . Long enough to ask me some questions. . . ."

"What are you going to say to them?"

"What did *you* say?"

"I showed them the door."

"You were a fool."

"I would have liked to see you before you spoke to them."

"Too late, now."

"Couldn't you come around here afterward?"

"I don't think I'll be in a fit state to drive."

"Have you been drinking?"

"No more than usual."

"Don't you think that at a time like this . . ."

"It's precisely at a time like this that one needs to put things out of one's mind."

"I'll come over."

"Over here? This evening?"

"It is absolutely necessary for me to speak to you."

"Necessary for whom?"

"For everyone."

"But for you most of all—isn't that right?"

"I'll be there in an hour. Try to retain a bit of composure and dignity until then."

"You'll have enough for both of us."

His brother-in-law's voice was devoid of emotion. Not a word about Adrienne, who must have been being cut up in the Medico-Legal Institute, not a word about what was happening to Kitten.

"I can listen to your questions now, chums. . . . I haven't much to tell you apart from what you've heard me say already. . . . I came back here to change before going out to dinner in town with some friends. . . . I expected to meet my wife. . . . A police inspector was waiting for me at the door. . . ."

"Was he the one who told you? . . . Here? . . ."

"No. . . . He wanted to know if I owned a pistol. . . . I said I did. . . . I looked for it in the drawer and it wasn't there any more. . . . The young man took me to his chief at the Criminal Police. . . ."

"Superintendent Roumagne?"

"That's the one."

"How long did he question you?"

"Less than an hour. . . . I don't know exactly. . . ."

"What was your reaction when you learned your wife had killed her sister?"

"I was shattered. . . . I can't understand it. . . ."

"Did they get on?"

"As well as any two sisters. . . ."

"Do you think it's a *crime passionnel*?"

"In a *crime passionnel* there's usually a third person. . . ."

"Exactly. . . ."

"You realize what that implies?"

They were silent.

"If there is one, I don't know who it is."

Some of the reporters exchanged knowing looks.

"Your glasses are empty."

He filled his and shoved the bottle into the hands of one of the photographers.

"Pour out for your friends, chum."

"Did you help your wife in her work?"

"I never even read her articles."

"Why? Didn't you think they were interesting?"

"On the contrary. I wanted her to feel free to write exactly what she felt."

"Did she never want to work for *Toi*?"

"She never even mentioned it to me."

"Were you very close?"

"Very."

"Do you think it was a case of premeditation?"

"I don't know any more about that than you do. . . . Any more questions . . . ? Tomorrow I may have some more ideas and I'll no doubt have got back to normal. . . . Just now my head is spinning and I'm waiting for my brother-in-law, who won't be very pleased to find you still here. . . ."

"He works for the Bank of France, doesn't he?"

"Exactly. . . . He's a very important man, and your editors-in-chief will advise you to treat him with respect."

"You didn't, on the telephone just now."

"That's an old habit of mine. My manners are atrocious."

They finally left, and Alain shut the door regretfully. He looked all around at the empty glasses and bottles, at the chairs that had been moved about, at the film wrappings scattered over the carpet. He was going to put the place in order before Blanchet's arrival, and he bent over to do it, then he straightened himself again, with a shrug of the shoulders.

He had heard the elevator stop, but he made Blanchet take the trouble to ring the bell like anyone else. Blanchet didn't make up his mind to do it right away. He waited for a moment in the hall, hesitating perhaps, or perhaps to compose himself.

The bell rang at last and Alain went slowly over to the door and opened it. He didn't hold out his hand. Nor did his brother-in-law; his coat was covered with tiny drops of water and his hat was wet.

"Are you alone?"

He seemed to be on his guard, as if, given the chance, he would have gone into the bedroom, the bathroom, and the kitchenette to make sure that there was no one listening.

"I couldn't be more alone."

Blanchet still didn't take off his coat or let go of his hat. He was looking at the glasses and the bottles.

"What did you say to them?"

"Nothing."

"You must have answered their questions. As soon as one agrees to let reporters in . . ."

"What would *you* have told them?"

The Blanchets, the father and the three sons, were big men, broad-shouldered and broad-chested, with just enough extra flesh to lend them an air of dignity. The father had twice been a Minister of State. One of the sons would be too, someday. They surveyed the world with the same condescending manner, and they must all have gone to the same tailor.

Adrienne's husband finally took his coat off and laid it on a chair and, since Alain was pouring a drink, hastened to protest:

"Not for me, thank you."

"It's for me."

After that there was a long, rather awkward silence. When he had set his glass down within reach of an armchair, Alain wandered mechanically toward the bay window, still coated with drops of water, through which the lights of Paris seemed to flicker. For a moment he found himself leaning his forehead against the glass as if to cool it, and he suddenly recoiled. Wasn't that how Kitten had stood in the apartment in Rue de l'Université, by Adrienne's body?

Blanchet had sat down at last.

"Just as a matter of interest, why did you have to come this evening?"

"I suppose because we have to come to an agreement."
"What about?"
"What we are going to say."
"We've already been questioned."
"As far as I'm concerned, I was only questioned superficially by a deputy superintendent who doesn't want to make things difficult for himself. Tomorrow or the day after that we'll be heard by a magistrate."
"That's what usually happens."
"What will you say?"
"That I don't know anything about it."
Blanchet stared at him with a look in which fear, anger, and disdain were mixed.
"Is that all?"
"What else can I say?"
"Has Jacqueline chosen a lawyer?"
"She's left that to me, as far as I can see."
"Whom have you picked?"
"I don't know yet."
"The lawyer's duty will be to defend his client."
"I should hope so."
"By whatever means he can."
"Naturally."
Alain was behaving this way on purpose. He had never been able to stand his brother-in-law, and his present attitude sickened him.
"How will he plead?"
"That's up to him, but I don't think he'll plead self-defense."
"Well, then?"
"Well, what do you suggest?"
Blanchet, shocked, said slowly:

"You seem to be forgetting that I am the husband of the victim."

"And I am the husband of a woman who is undoubtedly going to spend most of the rest of her life in jail."

"Whose fault is that?"

"Do *you* know?"

Another silence. Alain lit a cigarette and held his case out to Blanchet, who refused it with a shake of the head. How was he going to come through it without losing face? For he had only one idea in his head, or rather, one question that he was trying to find a way to ask.

"The superintendent asked me if we were a very close couple."

Alain could not refrain from giving him an ironic look.

"I said we were."

Alain was a bit annoyed with himself for letting this big, soft man flounder about without offering him any help. He was aware of the effort to speak calmly his brother-in-law must be making.

"I swore to him that Adrienne and I were as much in love as on the day we were married."

His voice had grown dull.

"Are you sure you won't have anything to drink?"

"No, nothing. He kept going on about the afternoons, I don't know why."

"Whose afternoons?"

"Adrienne's, of course. He wanted to know if she used to go out after lunch, and if she used to meet women friends. . . ."

"Did she?"

He hesitated.

"I don't know. We often had people in to dinner. We

dined a lot in town as well. Sometimes we would meet again at a cocktail party or an official reception. Adrienne used to take the children out for walks. She and the nurse took them to the Zoo."

"Did you tell the superintendent that?"

"Yes."

"Wasn't he satisfied with that?"

"Not altogether."

"What about you?"

At last, in an indirect way, came the first admission.

"I'm not either. . . ."

"Why?"

"Because I had a few words with Nana this evening."

She was the third or fourth nurse they had had since the children were born, and they called them all Nana, to make things easier.

"She wouldn't say anything at first, but she ended up crying and confessing to me that my wife didn't always stay at the Zoo. She used to go away, alone, and only came back to meet them at the end of the afternoon."

"Women have shopping, little things to do."

Blanchet swallowed his saliva noticeably as he looked Alain straight in the eyes, then he lowered his gaze.

"Tell me the truth."

"The truth about what?"

"You must realize that it is necessary, that it will be discovered one way or another. A murder has been committed and our private lives will be laid open to the public eye."

Alain hadn't yet made up his mind.

"Besides, I swear to you that I cannot . . ."

Blanchet couldn't finish his sentence and had to bury his face in his handkerchief. He had kept up appearances as long as possible. Now he was breaking down. Alain, out of a sense of decency, turned his head away, giving his brother-in-law time to regain his composure.

After that he had to come to the point. He emptied his glass before doing so. He didn't like Blanchet. He would never like him. In spite of that, he still felt pity for him.

"What do you want to know, Romain?"

It was the first time that evening that he had called him by his first name.

"Can't you guess? Were you . . . Were you and Adrienne . . ."

"Right! Put your handkerchief back in your pocket. Try, for once in your life, not to mix up your feelings and your sense of dignity. We'll talk man to man. Agreed?"

Blanchet sighed deeply and murmured:

"Agreed."

"First of all, get it into your head that I'm not calling your bluff as the magistrate would. What I'm going to tell you is the exact truth, even if I've sometimes happened to think otherwise. When I met Kitten it took me months to find out that I loved her. She would follow me around like a little dog. I got used to having her at my side. When we were apart for a few hours, on account of her work and mine, she would find a way to telephone me. We were sleeping together, and when I woke up during the night I used to stretch my hand over the space beside me until it touched her body."

"I didn't come here to talk to you about Kitten."

"Wait. This evening I can see things clearly. I think that, for the very first time, I can see things as they really are. The summer holidays came. She had to go and spend them with her parents."

"Was Adrienne in Paris at that time?"

"Yes, but I wasn't paying any more attention to Adrienne than to a canary that might have been in the room. She went away for a month, and after she'd been gone only a week I already felt terribly lonely. At night my hand only felt the sheet. In a restaurant or in a bar I would turn to my right and lean over to speak to her.

"That was the longest month of my life. I almost telephoned and asked her to come back, whatever the consequences."

Her father was a lecturer in literature at the University of Aix-en-Provence. The family owned a small villa at Bandol, and she spent every summer there.

He hadn't dared to go to Bandol himself, for he would have been too conspicuous.

"When she came back, I hadn't yet made up my mind. Then, suddenly, one night when we were with a crowd of friends in a night club on the Left Bank, I asked her if she would marry me. And that was it."

"That still doesn't explain to me . . ."

"Quite the contrary, it explains everything. I don't know if that is what people call love, but that's how things happened. We had a tough time for a while. Not all the time. There were good days and bad days. She couldn't get anyone to accept her articles. I hadn't yet thought of my magazine. As for Adrienne, she stayed in her room studying, like a good girl."

"Did she go out with you and Kitten?"

"Now and then. We didn't like the idea very much. Maybe she didn't like it either. She liked to stay in her corner, looking straight in front of her."

"Is that when . . ."

"Exactly. That's when it happened. Stupidly. By chance. I couldn't even say if it was she or I who made the first move. I was her sister's husband. In other words, her sister had a man of her own."

"Did you love her?"

"No."

"You're a cynic," Blanchet spat viciously.

"No. I told you we were going to talk man to man. She wanted to. Perhaps I wanted to, too, if only out of curiosity, to see what went on behind that closed face."

"Do you know now?"

"No. . . . Yes. . . . I think she was bored. . . ."

"So bored that after seven years . . ."

"No. We kept on seeing each other, like that, from time to time."

"What do you mean by 'from time to time'?"

"About once a week."

"Where?"

"That hardly matters."

"It matters to me."

"If you must picture everything in your own mind, that's your problem. In a furnished room on Rue de Longchamp."

"That's so sordid."

"I couldn't very well take her to Place Vendôme."

Place Vendôme, where Blanchet worked in the magnificent building of the Bank of France.

"She met you at the home of one of her girl friends. You went after her."

"Did she tell you everything?"

"I think so."

"Didn't she ask your advice, while she was at it?"

"Perhaps she did."

"You're a real louse."

"I know, but as far as that goes, there are several millions of us in the world. She married you."

"Did you go on meeting each other?"

"Not so often."

"Why not?"

"Because she had a house to look after. Then she was pregnant."

"By whom?"

"By you, you can be sure of that. I took every precaution."

"Lucky for you!"

"Let me get on with the story. I never mentioned it to Kitten. You must realize I often tell her about my affairs."

"You had others at the same time?"

"I'm not a government official and I haven't a reputation to keep clean. When I like a girl . . ."

"You have her and then you run and tell your wife about it."

"Why not?"

"And you say you and your wife are in love!"

"I didn't say any such thing. I said I missed her when she wasn't there."

"Did you miss my wife too?"

"No. That had become a habit. Maybe each of us was afraid to hurt the other's feelings by breaking it off. It came to that just the same, almost a year ago, two days before Christmas, the twenty-third of December."

"Thank you for being so precise."

"I must point out that nothing happened between us that day. We just drank a bottle of champagne."

"Didn't you see each other again?"

"At your house, at ours, at the theater. . . ."

"Never alone?"

"Never."

"Do you swear that?"

"If you want me to, though I don't really understand what difference that makes."

Little by little Blanchet had grown redder, then scarlet, and he seemed fatter and flabbier. When you got down to it, the Blanchets hid their flabbiness under well-cut clothes.

"How do you explain . . ."

"Are you sure you won't have anything to drink?"

"All right, I will have a whisky."

He stood up and remained standing in the middle of the studio, like an enormous apparition.

"Here's your drink!"

"This will all come out, won't it?"

"I'm afraid it will."

"Will you tell the magistrate what you've just told me?"

"I'll have to answer his questions."

"Do the reporters have any idea?"

"They didn't ask anything directly."

"I'm thinking of the children."

"No. The only thing you must do is be honest with yourself and look the truth straight in the face!"

"Almost a year since . . ."

"I'll swear to it again if you want me to."

"In that case I wonder why Kitten suddenly decided to . . ."

"To kill her sister. Let's speak plainly. I wonder why too. Now, she must have known that she was going to do it when she left the apartment. If she hadn't she wouldn't have taken my pistol, which, as far as I know, she's never touched before."

After a silence, Blanchet murmured:

"Unless there is someone else."

And he shot Alain a sly glance in which a certain amount of malice glinted.

"Have you thought of that?" he insisted.

"So much so that I'm still thinking of it."

"If Adrienne had another lover . . ."

Alain shook his head. His features, unlike Blanchet's, had grown clearer, harder.

"You've got it wrong. You're looking at things the wrong way around. Don't forget that your wife slept with me because, in her mind, I belonged to her sister."

"And that means . . . ?"

One would have said that the imposing brother-in-law was looking brighter. Even his body had taken on a clearer outline.

"It's unfortunate that Kitten began it. Adrienne paid her back. Only this time Kitten had had enough and pushed her right out of the picture."

"That doesn't seem to worry you very much. . . ."

Alain looked at him without moving a muscle, and Blanchet knew that he had gone too far. For a moment he was afraid. It was a physical sense of fear, a fear that he might be hit, that someone might hurt him.

"I'm sorry."

Alain stayed in his seat for a moment, glass in hand.

"So there you are," he said, putting an end to the matter.

Then, as he walked over to the bar:

"We're both done for."

"Will you tell all this to the magistrate?"

"No."

"You said, just a minute ago . . ."

"I will tell him what I know. The rest is just supposition and he'll get there soon enough on his own."

"Haven't you any idea?"

"Who it might be? No."

"But you usually saw your wife more than I saw mine."

Alain shrugged his shoulders. As if he paid any attention to what Kitten did or didn't do! All he asked of her was for her to be there, at his right elbow, within arm's reach and where she could hear him.

"Do you think she will talk?"

"She has refused to answer the superintendent's questions."

"But tomorrow?"

"I don't know anything about that. Personally, I don't give a damn who it might be."

They had no more to say to each other. They stayed there, wandering around the vast studio. Alain, in spite of all he had had to drink, felt quite sober.

"Aren't you going home?"

"Yes, of course. But I don't think I'll be able to sleep."

"Not me. I'm going to bury myself in sleep."

The other man put on his coat, looked for his hat, and wondered whether or not to hold his hand out to Alain, who was standing too far away from him.

"I'll see you soon. Or maybe tomorrow. The magistrate may decide to bring us together."

Alain shrugged his shoulders.

"Try to . . . not to make it too much a matter of Adrienne's . . . Don't judge her too hard. . . ."

"Good night."

"Thank you."

Blanchet went off awkwardly, sadly, closing the door behind him and, not bothering to call the elevator up, started to walk down the stairs.

Then, at last, Alain was able to let himself go, to let out a wild cry.

Chapter Three

HE had a disturbed night. Several times he half wakened—once not in his own place on the left side of the bed, but in Kitten's place. His stomach burned, and in the end he got up and went to the kitchen for some bicarbonate of soda.

When he heard a voice at his bedside it was barely daylight and the cleaning woman must have been shaking him by the shoulder to waken him. Her name was Madame Martin. She came every morning at seven o'clock and left at noon.

She gave him a hard look, her face stern.

"Your coffee is ready," she said coldly.

He had never accepted pity from others. He hated sentimental attitudes. He thought of himself as a realist and a cynic, and yet this morning he could have done with a bit of softness in his relationships with other people.

He went, without putting on his dressing gown, into the studio where the bright light battled with the grayness coming in from outside. The world on the other side of the immense bay window was bluish-green, the roofs were wet, and the sky, no longer covered with dramatic clouds as it had been the previous evening, was a dull, still, uniform shade of gray.

Ordinarily one could see the whole spread of the city from Notre-Dame to the Eiffel Tower. Today the panorama was limited to a few roofs and some lighted windows, although it was eight o'clock.

He gulped down his coffee, looking around the room. Chairs and armchairs had been put back in their places and the glasses and bottles had disappeared.

Madame Martin moved about the apartment doing her housework, her lips moving as if she were talking to herself. She was a woman of about fifty. The papers, which she usually brought up with her, were on a low table, but he didn't have the curiosity to look at them.

He didn't have a hangover, but he ached everywhere, mentally as well as physically, and his mind remained a blank.

"I had better tell you right away . . ."

This time her lips were not moving soundlessly. She was speaking.

". . . that this is the last morning I'll be working here."

She didn't give any explanation. He didn't ask for any, either. He poured himself a second cup of coffee and nibbled at a croissant, which stuck in his mouth. Finally he went over to the telephone and had a call put through to Saint-Illiers-la-Ville.

"Hello, Loulou?"

That was their cook, Louise Biran, the gardener's wife.

"Have you seen the papers?"

"No, not yet, but people have been coming by. . . ."

Her voice, too, sounded different.

"Don't believe everything people will be saying, or everything the papers will be printing. We don't know anything for certain yet. How is Patrick?"

He was five years old.

"He's well."

"Try to keep all this from him."

"I'll do my best."

"Has anything else happened?" He felt he had to ask that.

"Nothing apart from that."

"Could I ask you to make me some more coffee, Madame Martin?"

"You look as if you could do with it."

"I went to bed late."

"I thought that when I saw the state the apartment was in."

He went through and brushed his teeth, ran a bath, and then decided to take a cold shower. He didn't know what to do or where to go. Usually his movements in the morning had a precise rhythm. He had neglected to put the radio on as he would have done on another day, but he was afraid they would be talking about him and his wife.

He remembered the long, tunnel-like corridor at the end of which he had handed Kitten's suitcase over to a policeman. She too must be up by now. They were probably wakened very early, maybe even at six in the morning?

"Your coffee is ready."

"Thank you."

Wearing his dressing gown, he went to drink it, went over to the pile of newspapers at last, and read a headline:

YOUNG JOURNALIST HER SISTER'S MURDERESS

Then, in smaller letters:

SCANDALOUS AFFAIR PROBABLY DUE TO JEALOUSY

There was a bad photograph of Kitten crossing the forecourt of the Criminal Police building, her head hidden in her hands.

He didn't have the courage to read the article, or to look at the other morning papers. He had got up too early. Any other day he would have gone straight to Rue de Marignan, where he liked to be one of the first to arrive so that he could open the mail.

He had no desire to go to his office. He had no desire to do anything. Given a little encouragement, he would have gone back to bed and slept. It was reassuring to hear Madame Martin moving around the apartment, in spite of her hostility.

What had he forgotten to do? He knew that he had a full day ahead of him, but he was still vague about it, his head clouded.

Oh, yes! A lawyer! The one he knew best was the one who advised him about the magazine and about his record business. His name was Helbig, Victor Helbig, and it would have been difficult to guess his origins. His accent could just as well have been Czech as Hungarian or Polish.

A funny little man, middle-aged, fat, shining, his glasses as thick as magnifying glasses and his hair a flaming red.

He lived alone in a boardinghouse on Rue des Ecoles, surrounded by an unbelievable litter. None of this stopped him from being one of the most dreaded of lawyers.

"Hello, Victor? I haven't wakened you, have I?"

"You're forgetting that my day begins at six. I know already what you're going to ask me."

"You've read the papers?"

"I know enough about it to advise you to go to Rabut."

Philippe Rabut was the counsel who had defended the most notorious cases of the last twenty years.

"Don't you think that's admitting that it's a difficult case?"

"Your wife has killed her sister, hasn't she?"

"Yes, of course."

"She doesn't deny it?"

"She has admitted it."

"What explanation has she given?"

"None at all."

"That's a good thing."

"Why?"

"Because Rabut will tell her what line to take. How is this going to affect you?"

"What do you mean?"

"Your readers may not like the part you've played in it very much."

"I haven't played any part in it."

"Is that true?"

"It must be. It's almost a year since I've been near her sister."

"Phone Rabut. Do you know him?"

"Well enough."

"Good luck."

Alain had to look up Rabut's telephone number. He lived on Boulevard Saint-Germain. They had met frequently, at previews, at cocktail parties, at suppers.

A woman's voice, clear, almost sharp.

"This is Maître Rabut's office."

"This is Alain Poitaud," he said.

"One moment, please. I'll see if he's free."

He had to wait for quite some time. The apartment on

Boulevard Saint-Germain was vast. He had been there once, after a reception. The lawyer couldn't have gone through to his office yet.

"Rabut here. I was rather expecting you to ring."

"I thought of you right away. I almost called you last night, but I didn't want to disturb you."

"I got back very late from Bordeaux, where I was in court. Well, the case seems simple enough to me. What I can't understand is how a man like you could have got himself into such a situation. We won't be able to stop its being a scandal. Do you know if your wife has said anything?"

"According to Superintendent Roumagne, all she did was admit that she had fired the gun and refused to answer any other questions."

"That's something, anyway. What about the husband?"

"Do you know him?"

"I've met him."

"He says he knows nothing about it. Nor do I."

"Listen, old man, it won't be easy to put you in a good light."

"This hasn't happened because of me."

"Weren't you the sister's lover?"

"Not any longer."

"Since when?"

"Almost a year ago."

"Did you tell all this to the superintendent?"

"Yes."

"Did he believe that?"

"It's the truth."

"True or not, the public won't swallow that."

"I haven't called up about me, but about my wife. She'll be questioned again today."

"Of course. . . ."

"I would like you to agree to see her."

"I'm up to the ears in cases, but I can't refuse this one. Who is the magistrate who's been appointed?"

"I don't know."

"Are you at home? Stay there till I call you back. I'm going to try to find out what's going on at the law courts."

Alain telephoned his office.

"Is that you, Maud?"

One of his switchboard girls, with whom he had slept now and again.

"How are things with you, Chief?"

"Just the way you imagine, chum. Has Boris come in yet?"

"He's opening the mail. I'll put you through to him."

"Hello, is that you, Boris?"

"Yes, Alain. I thought you wouldn't be coming into the office this morning so I'm taking care of the mail."

Boris's surname was Maleski, and Alain had made him his editor. He lived in the suburbs, near Villeneuve-Saint-Georges, with his wife and four or five children. He was one of the few on the staff of *Toi* who weren't part of the "gang," one who went home when his work was finished.

"Is the mag out?"

"It's being sent out now."

"Any telephone calls this morning?"

"They're nonstop. The lines are all busy. You were lucky to get through."

"What are they saying?"

"It's mainly women. They want to know if it's true."

"If what's true?"

"That you were your sister's lover, which is what the papers are saying."

"I never said anything of the kind to the reporters."

"That doesn't stop them from drawing their own conclusions."

"What are you telling them?"

"That the investigation has hardly begun and that we know nothing."

Alain's confusion showed in his next question.

"What shall we do for the next issue?"

"Nothing. Well, since you're asking my opinion, I'll give it to you. No mention of the case at all. The issue as planned."

"You're probably right."

"You aren't too shaken up, are you?"

"That depends on the particular moment. I may come by Rue de Marignan sometime during the day. I don't think I have the guts to stay here by myself."

He was still wondering what he might do. The evening before, he had thought that his day would be so full that he wouldn't have any time to think, and here he was, feeling as lonely as if he were in a lighthouse, in his window-lined studio.

There were his parents. He had promised them that he would go and see them. They had lived in Place Clichy, not far away, for over fifty years, but he didn't often go to visit them.

He almost went out, then remembered in time that Rabut was going to telephone him. So he called the apartment in Place Clichy. He didn't care if Madame Martin overheard his phone calls. From now on he wouldn't have any secrets, any private life, for some of the newspapers wouldn't hesitate to tear his life to shreds.

"Hello, Mother? Yes, it's me. I would have come to see

you, but I don't know when I'll be able to. I'm at home. No. The cleaning woman is still here. She's just given notice. Why? Haven't you read the papers? What about Father? Didn't he say anything? Not a word? Is he in the office?"

His father was a dentist who began his working day at eight in the morning, seeing patients until eight in the evening, if not later.

He was a vigorous man, with gray hair in a crew cut and gray eyes, and he radiated such an air of serenity and gave such an impression of patience and understanding that his patients were ashamed of their aches and pains.

"What's that you're saying? . . . No, some things are true and some are not. In the next few days there will probably be a lot more which are not. I'll be around to see you as soon as I can. Give Father my love."

Madame Martin, duster in hand, was giving him a look of surprise, as if a monster such as he shouldn't have a mother and father.

What else could he do while he was waiting? He was chain-smoking. He thought about the law courts, about the Quai des Orfèvres, about the Central Police Station, about all the machinery that was going to be put in motion but which, for the moment, had left him stranded.

What would the women be doing, over there, during the empty hours, when they weren't being questioned?

It was ten o'clock. The phone rang and he rushed to answer it.

"Hello. Yes, it's me. . . ."

"Maître Rabut would like to speak to you."

"Hello! Hello! Rabut?"

"Yes. The magistrate has been named. It's Bénitet, quite a young man, thirty-five or thirty-six, a man who doesn't try to show off and who's very conscientious. He will be seeing your wife at eleven o'clock. I'll be there."

"Have the police finished with her?"

"Since she admits it and there's no mystery . . ."

"What about me?"

"I don't know when he'll want to see you. I'll know by the end of the morning. It's time I was getting over to the law courts. Where can I get in touch with you?"

"At my office. If I'm not there, leave a message with the switchboard girl."

Had he done everything he ought to have done? Not yet.

"How much do I owe you, Madame Martin?"

She took a slip of paper with figures penciled on it out of her apron pocket. It added up to a total of a hundred and fifty-three francs. He handed her two hundred-franc notes, and she made no attempt to give him any change.

"Leave the key with the concierge."

"If you don't find anyone else . . ."

"Thank you. I'll manage."

He walked downstairs. The staircase was wide, and it was a pity it had been spoiled by those leaded glass windows, which made it look old-fashioned or pretentious. There was only one apartment on each floor. A South American family lived on the second floor, very rich, with three or four children. The husband, after having studied in France, had headed his country's government and had been overthrown by a military coup.

On the first floor there were some offices belonging to an oil company. There was a consulate on the ground floor.

The concierge's room was more of a drawing room, and the concierge, Madame Jeanne, was a very dignified lady whose husband worked in one of the Ministries.

She avoided looking her tenant in the eye, trying to act as if nothing had happened.

"Poor Madame!" she murmured, finally.

"Yes."

"Heaven knows when she'll be coming back."

"I hope it will be soon."

He was getting used to it, in spite of his hatred of these ambiguous phrases.

"Tell me, Madame Jeanne, you wouldn't know of a cleaning woman, would you?"

"Is Madame Martin leaving you?"

"That's what she has just told me."

"I can understand her reasons, but I'm not sure that I approve of them. People don't always think what the consequences of their actions may be, do they? Especially men."

He didn't argue. She wouldn't be the only one to put the blame on him, to consider him the true culprit. What good would it do to argue?

"There is a young woman who isn't working and is looking for a job. You'll need someone for the mornings, I imagine?"

"It doesn't matter."

"What about wages?"

"I'll pay whatever she asks."

It was still drizzling, and most of the people in the street had umbrellas. The gates of Parc Monceau, at the end of the street, were blacker than usual and their gilded tips didn't glitter.

As he walked automatically toward his little red car he thought about Kitten's car. Where had it been left? Was it still at the Blanchets' door, on Rue de l'Université?

It upset him, for no particular reason, to think that the

car might be standing out like that, abandoned. He crossed over to the Left Bank and drove into Rue de l'Université. He saw the car standing, five hundred meters away from the mansion where the Blanchets had their first-floor apartment, shiny with rain. Two or three groups of people were standing by the grille in front of the house—sensation seekers, and possibly a few reporters too.

He drove toward Rue de Marignan and was swallowed up in the building where his offices, which had once occupied only the top floor, had nibbled away bit by bit until they had taken over almost the whole building.

The ground floor was devoted to the showrooms and pay desks. He took the elevator, got out on the fourth floor, and went along the corridors where the clacking of typewriters was heard everywhere through the open doors.

The building had been designed originally as apartments, and they had had to build dividing walls and knock down others. There were steps up and steps down, and one had to wind through a labyrinth of corridors.

From time to time he waved to someone, and eventually he reached the door of his office. Maleski was sitting in his chair.

He gave him a wave of the hand too and picked up the telephone.

"Put me through to my garage, chum. Yes, the one in Rue de Courcelles. There isn't a free line? Then call me back as soon as you can."

There was a mound of letters, as usual, and he glanced through some of them without really taking in what they said.

"Hello, yes. Hello, is that the Cardinet Garage? Is that

you, Benoît? This is Poitaud. Yes, thank you, old man. My wife's car is parked in Rue de l'Université. No. A bit farther down than the Ministry. I don't know if she left the key in it. Tell your mechanic to take anything he might need with him. Tell him to take it back to the garage. Keep it there, please. Yes. Give it a wash if you like."

Maleski was looking at him with interest. Everyone was going to watch him with interest, whatever he did, and he wondered how a man in his position ought to behave.

On the front page of a newspaper lying on the desk he saw a photo of himself, glass in hand, his hair disheveled.

The glass was going too far. They shouldn't have done that.

He forced himself to wander around the offices, shaking hands with various people, giving his usual:

"Hello, chum."

As far as appearances went, he was more at ease than they were, since they didn't know what to say to him or how to look at him. He went right upstairs, to the attic where they had torn down the walls to make the room where they set up the dummy. Julien Bour, one of the photographers, was leaning over a drawing board with Agnard, who did the dummies.

"Hello, chums."

He flicked through a pile of photographs, mainly nudes, in the style *Toi* had made its own. Chaste nudes or near-nudes.

"Everyone must see himself, or herself, in the magazine," he used to say to his original colleagues.

In the stories, too. Everyday stories. Exciting things that

could happen to anyone. The first poster, plastered on the walls of Paris several years earlier, had a finger pointing at the passers-by: You!

An enormous *Toi* that you couldn't escape.

"Listen, chums. We're not writing for everyone, but for each individual reader, and each reader must feel a part of it."

You . . . In your home . . . With you . . . In you . . .

He went downstairs again, and as soon as he went into his office he was handed the telephone receiver.

"Rabut," Maleski hissed.

"Hello. Have you any news? Has she said anything?"

"No. I can't talk to you where I am. Meet me at half past twelve in the canteen at the law courts. We'll have lunch there. I've been ordered by the magistrate to bring you to a confrontation at two o'clock."

"A confrontation with her?"

"Of course."

The lawyer hung up. He had been rather brusque, as if he were in a bad temper.

"I don't know if I'll be in this afternoon. Anyway, I won't have anything to do with the next issue. I'll leave that to you."

He went downstairs slowly. For years people had asked him:

"Where are you running off to now?"

Because he was always in a hurry and spent his days rushing from one place to another.

Today he was surprised to find himself walking like everyone else, and even walking slowly. His gestures were slower, too, even in lighting a cigarette. He glanced at the bar across the street, hesitated a moment, then crossed the street through the rain.

"A double scotch?"

He nodded and looked out of the window to avoid talking to the bartender. He had just enough time to get to the law courts without hurrying, and to find a parking place. Paris seemed heavy and sullen. Cars followed each other almost as if brought to heel. He had smoked two cigarettes before he got there, and he ended up parking quite far from Boulevard du Palais.

He knew the dark, shabby canteen quite well because he had covered the trials at the beginning of his career. Rabut was already a Maître of the Bench, and when he strode down the corridors or into the waiting hall, his robe swirling around him, its sleeves flapping like wings, the younger lawyers, and even those who were not so young, drew aside with respect.

Alain looked around for him among the tables where those on remand, who were going to be tried that afternoon, held whispered consultations with their defense counsels.

"Have you reserved a table?"

"I'm waiting for Maître Rabut."

"This way."

By the window, naturally. Alain watched him coming, a huge man, bull-necked, charging through the almost deserted courtyard as if it were the court itself. He carried no briefcase, no documents.

"Have you ordered yet?"

"No."

"I'll have the cold cuts and a half-bottle of claret."

"The same for me."

The lawyer's face could hardly be called smiling.

"How is she?"

"Cool, calm, and collected. She'll only have to show herself like that to the jury and she'll get the maximum."

"Is she still refusing to say anything?"

"When Bénitet asked her if she admitted having killed her sister, she answered simply 'Yes.' Then he asked her if when she had taken the Browning from your drawer in the morning she had already made up her mind what she was going to do. She said that she hadn't been quite sure, that she had made the decision later."

The cold cuts and wine were brought to the table, and they had to stop speaking for a few moments.

"Bénitet is a well-brought-up young man, and very patient. He treated her very gently. I think I would have given her a good slap if I'd been in his place."

Alain waited in silence for the other man to continue, but a spark of anger flashed in his eyes. He knew Rabut and the brutal streak that had a great deal to do with his success as a defense counsel.

"I don't know how she managed it, but she looked as if she had just come from the hairdresser's. She didn't have a hair out of place. She looked fresh and rested, and her suit hadn't a crease in it."

A green suit that she had had made three weeks earlier. She had gone out after he had the previous day, so that until that moment he had not known what she had been wearing.

"She sat there as if she were paying a social call. You know the old rooms, the ones right at the top of the building that haven't been modernized yet? That's where Bénitet's office is. Everything is covered with dust. There are piles of documents reaching halfway up the walls.

"In that atmosphere she looked like a lady on a visit, a lady who is afraid of getting dirty.

"He asked her over and over again why she had done what she did. She just answered:

" 'I have always hated my sister.'

"Naturally, he told her that that wasn't a good reason for killing her, and she replied:

" 'That depends.'

"I shall demand a psychiatric examination. Unfortunately, there isn't the slightest chance that she is insane."

Alain interrupted hesitantly.

"Kitten has always been a bit temperamental. I sometimes told her she was unpredictable, like a kitten purring by the fireside which will suddenly jump to the other side of the room for no apparent reason. That's why I nicknamed her Kitten."

Rabut looked at him impassively, chewing a slice of cold roast beef.

"That won't wash," he finally murmured, as if his companion had suddenly said something stupid. "The magistrate wanted to know if she had been motivated by jealousy. She didn't flinch, she didn't even open her mouth. From that moment on he wasn't able to get anything out of her except the silence which, by the end, was beginning to seem like contempt."

He took another mouthful. Alain ate too, not looking around. The world had never before seemed so small, and the next table could have been part of another world.

"The hardest bit to swallow was what came later. When your wife was on her way back to her cell . . ."

"Was she handcuffed?"

"Yes, in the corridors. That's the rule. I stayed with Bénitet for a moment, alone. He had just received the report from the police surgeon. Adrienne Blanchet didn't die at once, but lived for several minutes, four or five. . . ."

Alain still didn't understand. He looked impatiently at the lawyer, glass in hand.

"You probably know that the nurse, whom they call Nana, though her real name is Marie Poterat, was in the next room with the children. She heard some shouting at first and she had the good sense to take the children into the kitchen.

"At the very moment that she got into the corridor she heard the shots. The boy wanted to run and see. She had to drag them away almost by force, and she put them into the cook's care."

Alain, who knew the rooms and the people involved, reconstructed the scene in his mind automatically.

"You know, of course, that the kitchen is at the other end of the apartment. The nurse whispered to the cook not to let the children go out of the room.

"Knowing Bénitet, I am sure that he will send an inspector to check on these movements. When she got back to the bedroom door, Marie Poterat didn't go in right away, but stood listening. Since she didn't hear any more noise, she knocked.

"No one answered. Let's say that all that took three minutes. Now, when she went into the room your wife was standing up, her face pressed against the windowpane, and her sister was on the floor, lying half on the carpet, half on the bare boards, about a yard away from her little dressing table. A faint groan was coming from her parted lips."

And Rabut, spearing a piece of ham with his fork, went on:

"How can I defend that? She fires on her sister. That's

just great! It would have been better if it hadn't been her sister. Anyone else, but not her sister. People still believe that blood is thicker than water, and in Cain and Abel.

"Right, so it was jealousy. That's easy enough. But shooting her sister and leaving her in pain for four or five minutes without doing anything to help her and without calling out for help . . .

"Now, it'll be impossible to stop Marie Poterat from coming into court and being the chief witness for the prosecution.

"They'll make her describe the dying woman, then the woman who killed her just standing there by the window."

Alain had lowered his head. He couldn't think of anything to say. Rabut was right, of course, and yet it hadn't been quite that way.

He didn't know what the truth was, any more than anyone else did, but he was perhaps beginning to catch a glimpse of it.

"How long had you been her sister's lover?"

"I wasn't any more."

"How long had you been her lover?"

"About seven years. It wasn't the way you think. We had a sort of affection for each other."

"Just a minute. Did you sleep together, yes or no?"

"Yes, we did."

"Where?"

"In a furnished room in Rue Longchamp."

"That's bad."

"Why?"

"Mainly because nice people distrust places like that. They think they're shady, and they connect them, in their minds, with all kinds of vice."

Alain almost protested:

"It was all so innocent!"

He wasn't sure that Rabut would understand.

"When was the last time you went there?"

"December twenty-third, last year. So it was almost a year ago."

"Did your wife know?"

"No."

"Is she a very jealous woman?"

"She never said anything when I slept with any other woman."

"Did you talk to her about those times?"

"When I did, I told her."

"Did she never suspect your relationship with her sister?"

"Not as far as I know."

They looked at each other without saying anything. It looked as if things were turning out the same way as they had the previous evening with his brother-in-law.

"Do you imagine that there could be anyone else?"

"I've had to come to that conclusion."

"Now I'm asking you if you have any idea who it might be?"

"No, none."

"Did you and your wife spend a lot of time together?"

"I went out first in the mornings. She often had an article to write, and she did it at home. She used to telephone to Les Nonnettes, our country place, to talk to our son."

"How old is he?"

"Five."

"That's good. Good, or bad. That depends. And then what?"

"She almost always phoned me at the office at about eleven

o'clock to ask me where I was having lunch, and more often than not she would join me at the restaurant."

"And then?"

He had pushed away his plate and lit his pipe.

"She usually had to meet someone. Her specialty was interviewing celebrities passing though Paris. Not short pieces. Often they were real studies in depth which appeared in installments. After that she would phone me again, or come to meet me at the Clocheton, our bar on Rue de Marignan. There was always a crowd of about ten of us there between seven and eight o'clock."

"Did you have dinner alone together?"

"Not often."

"Did you get home late?"

"Hardly ever before one in the morning, more often between two and three."

Rabut, in a professional voice, pronounced:

"Not a real family life—juries, even if they permit themselves all kinds of escapades, lead family lives. You only have to mention what soup you had for dinner to bring tears to their eyes."

"We never have soup," Alain replied coldly.

"Tomorrow your wife will be transferred to La Petite Roquette. I will go to see her there. You can ask for a visiting permit too, but I doubt if you'll get it at this stage of the investigation."

"What are they saying in the papers?"

"Haven't you read them? They're being careful just now. You are a local celebrity here in Paris, and they don't dare go too far. Especially since your wife is a journalist too."

They stayed in the canteen another ten minutes, then

crossed the courtyard and climbed the steps. In the corridor of the Public Prosecutor's Office, prisoners, each handcuffed and standing between two policemen, were standing in front of numbered doors.

Near the end of the corridor they could see a group of reporters and photographers standing in front of one of the doors.

Rabut shrugged his shoulders.

"That's all we needed."

"I had them at my place last night."

"I know. I've seen the pictures."

Several flashes, the tide of reporters moved back, and the lawyer knocked two or three times at the door and entered with an air of authority, pushing Alain in in front of him.

"Forgive me, my dear fellow. I wanted to avoid meeting you at the door in front of the press. I'm afraid we are early."

"Three minutes."

The magistrate got up and motioned to them to sit down. The magistrate's clerk, seated at the end of the table, did not move.

The magistrate was fair-haired, with an athletic appearance and a placid temperament. He was wearing a well-cut dark gray suit, and he had a signet ring on one long, well-manicured hand.

"Have you filled in the picture for Monsieur Poitaud?"

"We had lunch together in the canteen."

"Monsieur Poitaud, I am sorry to have to subject you to a confrontation which may be upsetting to you, but I believe it is my duty."

Alain was suddenly surprised to find a lump in his throat and a hoarseness in his voice.

"I shall be very glad to see my wife again."

It had already been so long. It seemed to him that it had been an age since they had last seen each other, and it was difficult for him to picture her features exactly.

And yet it had only been the day before yesterday. When Madame Martin had come in and wakened him by shaking his shoulder he had got up, then he had drunk his coffee and eaten two croissants in the studio while looking over the papers. The headlines had been about the storm that was raging in the English Channel—two trawlers that had been sunk, the sea wall in Brittany that had been broken through, and the water that had flooded the cellars in some coastal villages.

He had dressed, as he did every other morning, and when he had bent over Kitten, who was still snuggled up in the bedclothes, she had opened her eyes.

"Good-by for now. Will you be calling me?"

"Not this morning. I told you that yesterday. I have to meet someone at the Crillon and have lunch with them."

"Well then, this afternoon?"

"This afternoon."

He had smiled as he stroked her hair. Had she smiled back? He couldn't remember.

"A cigarette?"

"Thank you."

He took one automatically. The waiting was embarrassing and they could hardly begin an ordinary conversation.

Luckily, there was a knock at the door. All three men rose. Only the clerk remained glued to his chair. Kitten came in, between two policemen who shut the door in the photographers' faces before removing her handcuffs.

"You may wait outside."

They were standing no more than two yards apart. She

was wearing her pale green suit, a finely embroidered blouse, and, on her brown hair, a funny little cap made of the same material as her suit.

"Please be seated."

She had looked at the magistrate first, then the lawyer. Finally she let her gaze rest on her husband's face.

It seemed to Alain that several expressions followed each other swiftly in his wife's eyes—first surprise, possibly at seeing his features hardened and his firm stare, then a spark of irony and also, he was certain, a trace of affection, or of friendship.

Before removing a file from a chair in order to sit down, she murmured:

"I must ask your forgiveness for having got you into this tiresome business."

He didn't flinch. He could find nothing to say and sat down. Only the lawyer, who was keeping himself in the background, separated one from the other.

The magistrate seemed staggered by what she had just said, and he took time to think before he spoke.

"Am I to understand, madame, that your husband has nothing to do with what happened on Rue de l'Université?"

Rabut wriggled in his chair, afraid of what she might say.

"I have nothing to add to what I have already said."

"Do you love your husband?"

"I suppose so."

She did not look at him. She seemed to be looking for a cigarette. The three men sitting around her were all smoking. Bénitet understood her look and held out his pack to her.

"Were you jealous?"

"I don't know."

"As far as you know, has your husband had intimate relations with your sister?"

She turned to look at Alain for the first time, very sure of herself, and murmured:

"He should know that better than I do."

"I am asking you the question."

"I have nothing to say."

"When did the idea of killing your sister first come into your head?"

"I don't know."

"Yesterday morning? I must remind you that before you left your apartment you took a gun from its place in your husband's drawer."

"That is so."

"With what intention?"

She repeated her words:

"I have nothing to say."

"You are beginning to behave the way you did this morning, again."

"I fully intend to have the same attitude."

"In order to shield someone?"

She merely shrugged her shoulders.

"Was it because of your husband?"

"I have nothing to say."

"Do you regret your action?"

"I don't know."

"Will you take an oath to that effect?"

"That depends."

"On what?"

"It doesn't matter."

"I wonder, Maître, if you have any advice to give your client?"

"That will depend on what she may tell me when I see her alone."

"You may see her tomorrow for as long as you feel necessary."

He stubbed out his cigarette in an ashtray advertising some product or other.

"And now you, Monsieur Poitaud. I will authorize you to ask your wife any questions you would like to ask her."

Alain raised his head and looked at the face turned toward him. She was merely waiting, her expression betraying no emotion whatever.

"Listen, Kitten . . ."

He didn't say any more. He didn't have anything to say either. He had wanted to say her name, rather like an incantation, hoping to strike some kind of spark.

They remained a long time looking at each other, she waiting patiently, he hunting for words he couldn't find.

It was a little like that children's game where two people look at each other and wait to see who will be the first to smile.

Neither one smiled. Neither one laughed. Alain was the first to yield. He turned toward the magistrate.

"No. I have no questions."

They were all upset except the woman. The magistrate regretfully pushed a button. An electric bell rang on the other side of the door and the door opened.

"Take Madame Poitaud back to her cell."

For she was still "Madame." Soon she would be "the prisoner," and finally she would become "the accused."

Alain noticed that it had grown dark, that they had had to put on the lights. He heard the clank of the handcuffs, the sound of high heels clicking along the floor, the flash-guns of the photographers.

Rabut must have opened his mouth once the door had shut again, because the magistrate asked him:

"Do you wish to say something else, Maître?"

"No. I shall be seeing her tomorrow."

The journalists had gone when they left, and the corridor was almost deserted.

Chapter Four

He stood there, alone in the drizzle, in front of the railings of the law courts, without the slightest idea of where to go. He refused to admit to his confusion, and he was forcing himself to believe that, given a little time, a pencil, and some paper, he could put his ideas in order.

He had always tried to make himself cynical, even in childhood, even at school, where he had already had his own little group around him, and when he had failed his *baccalauréat* he had pretended to be delighted about it.

"Only idiots get diplomas!"

He walked across the street and went into a bar.

"A whisky . . . A double . . ."

That was a habit he had grown into and one which his friends had copied. Most of them drank a little less than he did, because they couldn't hold as much as he could, or because they felt so terrible the next day.

It wasn't a whisky-drinker's bar. There was only one bottle on the shelves. The other customers were drinking coffee or glasses of white wine.

"Still, Alain, you must choose a career."

How many times had his mother said that to him? He used

to wander about the streets and hang about cafés. Perhaps he was as worried as she was, but he made it a point of honor not to show it.

"I will never agree to living the life of a slave."

A slave like his father, who spent twelve or fourteen hours a day messing about with bad teeth.

Like his father's father, who had been a country doctor until he had died of heart failure, at the wheel of his car, at the age of seventy-one.

Like his other grandfather, the confectioner, who had made sweets and toffees in an overheated basement all his life, while his wife served behind the counter.

"You see, Mother, there are two kinds of people: those who get pushed around and those who do the pushing."

He had added, defiantly:

"I'm going to be one of the ones doing the pushing."

After spending six months doing nothing, he had joined the army and spent three years in Africa.

He ought to go to Place Clichy to see his parents. His father had never interfered with what he had wanted to do. He had let him do what he liked, no doubt because he had realized that any intervention would turn Alain into a rebel.

Why had Kitten asked his forgiveness? That had been the only thing she had said to him. She had not been in the least moved.

He almost asked for another drink. It was too early for that. He left the café and went to his car, which was parked quite a distance away.

He slid behind the steering wheel and started the car. Where would he go? He knew everyone, he called hundreds of people "chum." He was a man who had made his mark in the world, he had made a lot of money. He had always known that he wouldn't be one of the "pushed around."

Toi had a circulation of about a million. His records were selling well. He was about to put out a magazine for younger readers, boys and girls of ten to fifteen.

To whom could he talk at this particular moment, to whom could he speak freely? And anyway, did he really want to speak freely? Did he really want to understand?

He went back to Rue de Marignan, because he needed to be surrounded by people who were his subordinates, the people he called his chums. He had given Kitten a name too, rather like branding cattle in the Wild West. He had given Adrienne a name too.

Something in him had snapped, he didn't know quite what, and he was beginning to be afraid.

There was a queue, mainly of women, at one of the little windows in the hall. They had come for the competition. One always needed a competition to keep the female readers on tenterhooks, and then one could say what one liked in the rest of the magazine.

He walked upstairs. The first floor was the only floor that didn't belong to him. It was occupied by an import-export firm. He had bought up the lease. In six months the whole building would belong to him, and he planned to rebuild it.

He was thirty-two years old.

Who had asked him about Les Nonnettes? Who had asked him if he had ever lived a family life with Kitten?

Never! At that tumble-down building which they had rebuilt, half farmhouse, half manor house, every weekend was one long party, and one didn't always know, in the morning, who was sleeping in what bed or on what divan.

"Hello, Boris."

Maleski was watching him, rather as if he was trying to discover just how hard he was taking it.

"Your brother-in-law phoned. He wants you to call him back."

"At home?"

"No, at Place Vendôme."

"He's a pompous fool."

He had said that before. He hated pompous people. Fools irritated him.

"Get me the Bank of France, chum. Yes, the head office, on Place Vendôme. Ask for Monsieur Blanchet."

Gagnet, the editorial staff secretary, came in holding some papers.

"Am I in the way?"

"No, not at all. Are those for me?"

"I wanted to show Boris an article that's giving me a bit of trouble."

This week Alain would have nothing to do with it. It was Thursday. Thursday the nineteenth of October. That was easy to remember because everything had started on Tuesday the seventeenth, two days before. At this time on that day he had been sitting at his desk, where Boris was sitting now. Then he had gone to the printer's on Avenue de Châtillon, and there had been nothing of greater importance in his mind than the issue of *Toi* that was about to appear.

"Monsieur Blanchet can speak to you now."

He pressed a button.

"Alain speaking."

"I called you because I'm wondering what to do. Adrienne's father has arrived in Paris. He is staying at the Hôtel Lutétia."

Just like any good provincial or foreign intellectual!

"He wants to see us both."

"Why both of us?"

"It's a question of his two daughters, isn't it?"

One dead, the other in prison!

"I have invited him here to have dinner with me this evening, as a precaution, since we can hardly go out to a restaurant. I told him I would telephone and confirm the arrangement after I had got in touch with you."

"At what time?"

"At about eight o'clock."

There was a short silence.

"They are bringing Adrienne's body back tomorrow morning. The funeral will take place on Saturday.

Alain hadn't thought about a funeral.

"That's all right about this evening."

"Have you seen her?"

"Yes."

"Didn't she say anything?"

"She asked my forgiveness."

"Yours?"

"You may find that surprising, but that's what she said."

"What does the magistrate think?"

"He hasn't told me what he thinks."

"And Rabut?"

"He's not very happy."

"Has he agreed to defend her?"

"The minute he was asked . . ."

"I'll see you this evening."

"Till this evening, then."

He looked at Boris and Gagnon, who were arguing in low voices about the article. He very nearly chose one of the typists or switchboard girls with whom he had already slept to go and make love to, anywhere, it didn't matter where.

People have conventional ideas, and the girl might have said no.

"See you soon, maybe tomorrow."

It was only four o'clock. He went into the Clocheton.

"A double?"

He didn't have any desire to drink. It was a reflex action.

"What's that? Oh, yes, chum."

"Have you seen her?"

The bartender knew Kitten, of course. Everyone knew Kitten, since they always saw her, sitting or standing, a little to the right of his elbow.

"Less than an hour ago."

"She's not too depressed, is she?"

"All she needs is a glass of good whisky."

The other man didn't know whether to smile or not. Had Alain shocked him? Too bad! He was used to shocking people. He did it on purpose. Or rather, he had done it on purpose for so long that now it was second nature to him.

"It looks as if the rain might stop."

"I hadn't noticed it was raining."

He spent a quarter of an hour leaning on the bar, then got into his car again. He drove back up the Champs-Elysées under a sky that was indeed brightening, turning a horrible yellow, like a boil.

He turned into Avenue Wagram, then Boulevard de Courcelles. He didn't turn left to go to his own place. He parked the car right at the top of Boulevard de Batignolles.

The neon signs had just come on. He knew Place Clichy in all its guises—black with people going into or coming out of the métro entrances, or deserted at six in the morning, when it belonged only to the street sweepers and the vagrants; under the sun, under the snow, in the rain, in winter, in summer, at any time.

He knew it so well that he was sick of the sight of it, because he had watched it from his window for eighteen years. Seventeen, because he had been too small to reach the window the first year, and he hadn't been walking then.

He went into a narrow passageway between a bistrot and a shoeshop. A board that had always been exactly the same bore the legend:

OSCAR POITAUD
DENTAL SURGEON
(*2nd floor, right*)

Every day, coming home first from kindergarten, then from primary school, and then from the *lycée,* he had seen that board as he passed, and he hadn't been eight years old when he had vowed that he would never be a dentist, whatever happened.

He scorned the elevator that broke down two or three times a week, trapping the occupants between floors.

He climbed the old, bare stairs, went past the *entresol,* where there was a chiropodist's, then past the first floor, where each room served as an office for a different business. Shabby businesses, just keeping on the right side of the law.

As far back as he could remember, there had always been at least one moneylender in the building. Not always the same one, or even on the same floor.

He felt nothing. His childhood aroused no emotional feelings in him—quite the reverse. He hated the memory of his childhood. He would have wiped it out as one would wipe a blackboard, if he could have done so.

He didn't hate his mother. She was almost as much of a

stranger to him as his aunts, whom he used to see once a year when visiting the family home in Dijon.

His mother's family name was Parmeron, and this name, prefixed by Jules, was painted on the sign above the confectioner's shop. The aunts were all out of the same mold, small and broad, with serious faces and slightly sugary half-smiles.

He went into the dining-cum-living room. The real living room was kept as a waiting room for patients. He recognized the smell, and heard the drill droning in his father's office.

His mother was wearing an apron which she hurriedly took off when she went to open the door. He had to bend down to kiss her on both cheeks, for he was much taller than she.

She didn't dare to look him in the face, and as they went into the dining room filled with heavy furniture she murmured:

"If you only knew how upset I am!"

He restrained himself from saying:

"What about me, then?"

That wouldn't have been kind.

"When your father saw the front page of the paper this morning he couldn't finish his breakfast."

At least he was shut up in his office, with a patient coming in every quarter of an hour.

"Rinse your mouth . . . Spit . . ."

When Alain was a little boy he used to put his ear to the door.

"Will it hurt?"

"No, of course not! If you don't think about it, it won't hurt."

In that case, all Alain had to do was not to think about it.

"How could she have done such a thing, Alain? A woman who always seemed so sweet."

"I don't know, Mother."

"Do you think she was jealous?"

"She didn't seem to be."

She looked at him at last, apprehensively, as if she were afraid that she would find he had changed.

"You don't look too tired."

"No. Of course, it only hits you on the second day."

"Did they come to your office to tell you?"

"To the apartment. There was an inspector waiting there for me. He took me to the Quai des Orfèvres."

"But you hadn't done anything, had you?"

"They still had to question me."

She went to the sideboard and took out an already opened bottle of wine, for a stirrup cup, so to speak. It was a tradition. No matter who came to see her.

"Do you remember, Alain?"

"Remember what, Mother?"

One of the pictures on the wall, a dull, flat picture, was of cows in a field, standing by a rustic gate.

"What I always used to tell you. You only wanted to do what *you* felt like. You never learned a real profession."

He decided not to mention the magazine to her, as she considered it an invention of the devil.

"Your father doesn't say anything, but he must be sorry he was so soft with you. He let you do what you liked and excused himself by saying:

" 'He'll find his own way by himself, you'll see. . . .' "

She sniffed and wiped her eyes on the corner of her apron. He was sitting on an embossed leather chair. She was standing. She always stood.

"What's going to happen now, do you think?"

"There'll be a trial."

"Will you be mentioned?"

"Naturally."

"Tell me, Alain. Don't lie to me. You know I can always tell when you're lying. It's because of what you did, isn't it?"

"What do you mean?"

"You were having an affair with the sister, and when your wife found out . . ."

"No, Mother. This has nothing to do with me."

"Was there someone else?"

"There may well have been."

"Someone you know?"

"It's possible. She hasn't told me about it."

"Don't you think she's a bit mad? If I were you, I would insist that she have a psychiatric examination. She was a sweet girl, a nice girl. I really liked her, and I thought she was really fond of you. Still, I always felt there was something wrong."

"What?"

"It's hard to say. She wasn't like everyone else. One of my sisters-in-law, Hortense, you never knew her, was like that. She had the same look, the same gestures, and she had to be put into an institution."

She pricked up her ears.

"Wait here. The patient is leaving. Your father will come in to see you before the next one goes in."

She went toward the hall. When she came back a moment later she was followed by a square-built man, his gray hair in a crew cut.

He didn't kiss his son. Even when Alain was a boy he had

rarely kissed him. He put his hands on Alain's shoulders and looked him straight in the eyes.

"Is it hard for you?"

Alain forced himself to smile.

"I can take it."

"Did you suspect anything?"

"No, nothing."

"Have you seen her since?"

"I saw her a little while ago, in the magistrate's office."

"What has she to say?"

"She refuses to answer any questions."

"There's no doubt that she did it?"

"None at all."

"Have you any ideas?"

"I prefer not to look for any."

"And the husband?"

"He came to see me last night."

"What about her parents?"

"Her father has come to Paris. I'm having dinner with him in a little while."

"He's a good man. . . ."

The two men had met only two or three times, but they had got on well together right away.

"Keep your chin up, boy. I don't have to tell you that this house is always open to you, and that we are always here. I have to get back to work. The factory."

That was what he called his office. He patted Alain on the shoulder once more and went toward the door, his white coat flapping against his legs. Why had he always bought his coats too long?

"You see! He doesn't say anything, but he is overwhelmed. The Poitauds have never been ones to show their feelings.

When you were just a little boy you refused to cry in front of me."

The red wine was making him feel sick and he stopped his mother from pouring him a second glass.

"No thank you. I have to go."

"Have you got anyone to take care of you?"

"The cleaning woman."

"Of course, you usually eat out. Doesn't that upset your stomach?"

"It's holding up."

He stood up, his head touching the chandelier, bent over his mother, and kissed her on both cheeks. He was almost at the door when he turned.

"Listen, Mother. I can't stop you from reading the papers. But don't be upset by what they may say. They don't always tell the truth. I should know. I'll see you soon."

"You'll tell us what's happening, won't you?"

"Yes, I will. I promise."

He went down the steep stairs. That was over. He owed it to them. There was a real mist rising from the damp streets now, haloing the street lamps and the neon signs.

A boy with a pile of newspapers under his arm ran past. Alain didn't have enough curiosity to buy one.

He had to go somewhere. He had to be somewhere. But where?

Everyone around him was walking quickly, bumping into each other, as if they had some goal to reach in a tremendous hurry. He remained standing at the edge of the sidewalk, in the damp air, and lit a cigarette.

Why?

Albert, a manservant in a bartender's white jacket, took

his coat and showed him into the drawing room. Blanchet was standing there alone, wearing a black suit. He must have thought that it was his father-in-law arriving, and his expression changed when he saw Alain.

"I seem to be the first to arrive."

He was walking rather stiffly, as he had had a lot to drink during the afternoon. His eyes were glazed and red, a fact that didn't escape Blanchet's notice.

"Sit down."

The drawing room was too high-ceilinged, too vast altogether, for the two of them. The antique furniture must have come from a National Furniture Repository, and the huge crystal chandelier couldn't even begin to light the corners of the room.

They looked at each other. They did not shake hands.

"He'll be here any minute now."

Fortunately, he did arrive. They heard the bell ring, Albert's footsteps, the door opening. Finally the manservant showed in a man who was as tall as all the Blanchets, but very thin and slightly stooped, with a pale, fine-featured face.

His bony hand grasped Alain's firmly. Still saying nothing, he went over to his other son-in-law to shake his hand. After that he was overcome by a fit of coughing and covered his mouth with his handkerchief.

"It's nothing to worry about. My wife is in bed with bronchitis. The doctor wouldn't let her come with me. It's probably better that way. As for me, I just have a cold that keeps hanging on."

"Shall we go into my study?"

An Empire study, just as official as the drawing room.

"What can I offer you, Monsieur Fage?"

"Anything. A glass of port, perhaps."

"What about you, Alain?"

"Scotch."

Blanchet hesitated and shrugged his shoulders. André Fage, his face still youthful and free from lines, his gray hair combed back, and his features finely drawn, was the perfect "intellectual type" as it is popularly imagined. One could tell that he was a calm, gentle person.

After Albert had filled their glasses, Monsieur Fage looked at Alain and Blanchet in turn, then said:

"There you are in the same boat, and I have lost my two daughters. I wonder which of them I grieve for the more. . . ."

His voice was thickened by controlled emotion. He looked at Alain again.

"Have you seen her?"

They met so rarely that they hardly knew each other.

"This afternoon, at the magistrate's."

"How did she seem?"

"I was surprised to find her so calm, so self-controlled. She had dressed carefully, and you would have thought she was paying a social call."

"That's just like my Jacqueline! She has always been like that. Even when she was a very little girl, when she felt at a loss she would hide in a corner of the apartment, in a cupboard perhaps, and she wouldn't come out until she had control of herself again."

He sipped his port and put down the glass.

"I have avoided reading the papers, and I shan't read them again for quite some time."

"How were you told about it?"

"By the police superintendent. He came himself, and he

was very good about it. My wife is in bed, as I've already said. We spent part of the night talking about it in whispers, just as if it had happened at home."

He looked around.

"Where *did* it happen?" he asked Blanchet.

"In the bedroom, or rather in the little dressing room that opens off it."

"Where are the children?"

"They're having dinner with Nana in the playroom."

"Do they know?"

"Not yet. I told them that their mother had had an accident. Bobo is only six and Nelle just three."

"There will be plenty of time to tell them."

"They are bringing her back here first thing tomorrow morning. The funeral will be on Saturday at ten o'clock."

"A church service?"

He was not a religious man, and his daughters had been given a secular education.

"There will be a mass and prayers of intercession, yes."

Alain felt so out of place that he wondered what he was doing there. And yet he had always liked his father-in-law and felt they could have been friends. Hadn't Fage written his thesis on the relationship between Baudelaire and his mother?

He listened to the others without feeling any need to intervene. They were different, especially Blanchet. They might have been living on some other planet.

Or was it he who was not like other people? Yet he was married, he had a child, a house in the country. He worked from morning till night, often well into the night.

It seemed to him that the lighting was very dim. Had it become a mania, since the previous evening, to find that no place was bright enough? He felt as if he were imprisoned in a chiaroscuro and that words were only getting to him through some filtering material.

"Dinner is served."

Albert was wearing white gloves. The table was big enough for a dozen people and was covered with silver and crystal, with an épergne full of flowers in the center. Had Blanchet thought of the flowers? Did he do these things automatically in spite of what he felt inside?

They were seated rather far apart, Fage in the middle, bent over his soup.

"Do they know if she felt any pain?"

"The doctor says not."

"When she was very small I used to call her the Sleeping Beauty. She didn't have Jacqueline's vivacity, or her charm. You might even have said she was a bit stupid."

Alain couldn't help remembering the way Adrienne had looked at certain moments and comparing them with the portrait painted by her father.

"She used hardly to play at all. She would stay seated by a window for an hour, watching the clouds go by.

" 'Aren't you bored, dear?'

" 'Why would I be bored?'

"Sometimes my wife and I were worried by that calm, which we took to be listlessness. Doctor Marnier reassured us.

" 'Don't worry about it. When she comes out of it, you will find it hard to hold her down. That child is leading an intense inner life.' "

There was a long silence. Blanchet took advantage of it to have a fit of coughing, though not as long as his father-in-law's had been. Fillets of sole were served.

"Later on they grew jealous of each other, although we did all we could to avoid it. I believe it is just the same in every family. It began when Jacqueline was allowed to go to bed an hour later than her sister.

"For months Adrienne refused to go to sleep. She was dropping with exhaustion, but she held out, and we ended up by compromising. They would go to bed at the same time, halfway between Adrienne's bedtime and Jacqueline's."

"That was unfair to Jacqueline," Alain remarked.

It felt odd to him to say that name, not to say "Kitten."

"I know. When you have children, it isn't possible to be fair."

At thirteen Adrienne had insisted on being dressed like her sister, who was sixteen, so that she had looked like a young lady even at that age.

"Two years after that she was smoking. My wife and I were as liberal as possible. With both girls. It would have been worse if they had rebelled."

He looked blankly into space. Suddenly reality hit him and he added in a faint voice:

"What could have been worse?"

He looked at his two sons-in-law.

"I wonder which of you I'm sorrier for."

Frowning, he began to eat again. There was no noise but the sound of silver on china.

Albert took away their plates, served the young partridge, and refilled their glasses, this time with Burgundy.

Blanchet said:

"I went to see her, down there."

"Down there" was the Medico-Legal Institute. Metal shelves, like racks, in which the bodies were laid in rows.

Her father murmured:

"I wouldn't have had the courage to do that."

Was all this really happening? Wasn't it a stage set on which three actors were playing their parts in slow motion? The silences were frequent and unbearable. For a moment Alain wanted to shout, to gesticulate wildly, to do anything, to throw his plate onto the floor, for example, anything to bring them back to life.

They weren't talking about the same women. For Fage they were still babies, little girls, adolescents.

"When my children were born, I dreamed of the day when they would confide in me, when I would be their friend and could perhaps be helpful to them."

He thought for a moment, then turned to Blanchet.

"Did Adrienne talk to you a lot?"

"No, not a lot. She didn't feel a need to give of herself."

"What was she like with your friends?"

"She was a good hostess, and yet she never put herself forward. One hardly knew she was there."

"You see! She stayed the same. She led an inner life and was incapable of communicating with others. What about Jacqueline, Alain?"

He hesitated, since he didn't know what to say. He didn't want to hurt this man who was taking the blow dealt him by fate so much to heart.

"Kitten . . . That's what I called her. . . ."

"I know."

"Kitten had to keep her personality intact, and that's why she went on working. I was never allowed in that world, and she never asked for my help or advice. Part of the day belonged to her alone. The rest of the time she never left my side for a minute."

"That's funny, your saying that. I can see her now, sitting

in a chair in my study doing her homework. She used to come in so quietly that I was surprised, when I looked up, to find her sitting opposite me.

" 'Do you want to speak to me?'

" 'No.'

" 'Are you sure you don't want to talk to me?'

"She would bow her head. She only wanted to be there, nothing more, and I would get on with my work.

"When she decided to finish her studies in Paris instead of staying in Aix, I understood quite well that she didn't want to be the professor's daughter."

That was not true! Kitten had decided to launch out on her own.

"Naturally, Adrienne followed suit, so my wife and I were left alone at the very moment when we had hoped we would most be enjoying the company of our children."

He looked at one, then at the other.

"You were the ones to enjoy it."

What had they had for dessert? Alain didn't remember. The dinner over, they followed Blanchet into the study, where he handed them a box of Havana cigars.

"Coffee?"

Alain didn't dare to look at his watch. The Empire clock had stopped.

"I never interfered in their affairs. I didn't insist on their writing us more often or giving us more details of what they were doing. Did they still see each other after they were both married?"

Alain and Blanchet looked questioningly at each other. Blanchet said:

"Jacqueline and her husband sometimes came to dinner. Not often."

"About two or three times a year, on the average," Alain added.

His brother-in-law took that as a reproach.

"You know you were welcome to come at any time."

"We were each busy with our own circle of friends."

"They used to telephone each other. I think they used to meet in town for tea, too."

Alain would have sworn that that had happened only twice in seven years.

"We used to meet at the theater, or in a restaurant."

Fage looked at them both in turn, his expression revealing nothing of his feelings.

"You spend your weekends in the country, Alain, don't you?"

"Sometimes part of the week, too."

"How is Patrick?"

"He's getting to be a big boy now."

"Does he know his cousins?"

"They've seen each other."

Fage didn't ask how many times. It was better that way. He couldn't be feeling at his ease either in that house which was only a stage set, giving away nothing of the daily life of those who lived there.

"Hasn't she said why she did it?"

They had returned abruptly to the main subject.

Alain shook his head.

"Does neither of you know?"

An even heavier silence answered his question.

"Perhaps Jacqueline will decide to speak."

"I doubt it," sighed Alain.

"Do you think they'll allow me to see her?"

"I believe so. Go and see Bénitet. He's a good man."

"Will she speak to *me*?"

He doubted this so obviously that he had a sad smile. His complexion was very pale, his lips were almost colorless, and, in spite of his size, he seemed frail.

"I believe I can understand her, when I think about it."

He looked at them again. It seemed to Alain that there was more sympathy in the look Fage shot at him than in the one he gave Blanchet. Sympathy, yes, but also curiosity, even a certain mistrust.

Finally he sighed:

"Perhaps it's as well it happened this way. . . ."

Only Blanchet was smoking a cigar. The sweet smell made the atmosphere heavy. Alain was on his fourth or fifth cigarette. Fage wasn't smoking. He took a box from his pocket and took out a pill which he put in his mouth.

"Can I get you some water?"

"No, don't trouble. I'm used to it. It's a drug to activate the circulation. Nothing serious."

What else was there for them to say? Blanchet opened the cupboard that was used as a liqueur cabinet.

"What can I offer you? I have a very old Armagnac. . . ."

"Nothing, thank you."

"Nothing, thank you."

In his disappointment Blanchet, with his big, soft body, looked like a spoiled child.

He turned toward Fage.

"I'm sorry not to have asked you this sooner. Wouldn't you feel better staying here than at the hotel? We have a guest room."

"No, thank you. They know my little ways at the Lutétia, after all these years. I used to stay there, as did all my friends and my professors, when I was a student visiting Paris. The décor is a little faded, like me. . . ."

He got up, stretching out his thin body like an accordion.

"I must go back now. Thank you both."

He had not let out a hint of what he thought. He had hardly asked them any questions. Perhaps it was only his good taste.

"I must go too," Alain declared.

"Won't you stay for a little?"

Did Blanchet want to speak to him? Or was he afraid of what Alain might say to his father-in-law?

"I must go to bed."

Albert held out their coats.

"The body will be laid out in the drawing room tomorrow."

The drawing-room doors were open and the room seemed inordinately long. Was the father imagining the same décor with the black draperies and the bier, alone in the center of the room, surrounded by candles?

"Thank you, Roland."

"Good night, Monsieur Fage."

Alain followed his father-in-law down the stairs. Their footsteps crunched on the gravel of the drive where the trees, pitch-black, were dripping after the rain.

"Good-by, Alain. . . ."

"I have my car here. I can drive you back."

"No, thank you. I need to walk."

He looked at the deserted street, still shining wet, and sighed as if to himself:

"I need to be alone."

Alain shivered, shook the bony hand quickly, and jumped into his car.

He had a new weight on his shoulders. He felt as if he had just been given a lesson, and he felt like a little boy.

He too should have wanted to be alone, but he didn't have the courage. He drove off wondering where he could find somebody, anybody, to whom he could call:

"Hello, chums!"

They would make room for him. The waiter would bend over:

"A double, Monsieur Alain?"

He was ashamed. It was too strong for him.

Chapter Five

He could hear a ringing, very distant and yet at the same time very close, then a silence, then the ringing again, as if someone were sending him signals. Who could be signaling him? He was unable to move, for he was at the bottom of a pit. He must have had a blow on the head, it ached so terribly.

This went on for a long, long time, until he realized that he was in his own bed. Then he got up, staggering.

He was quite naked. He saw red hair spread out on the other pillow. He now realized that someone was ringing the doorbell, and he looked for his dressing gown, found it on the floor, and put it on with some difficulty.

As he walked through the studio, he saw that dawn had hardly broken over Paris. There was just a yellow line in the distance, beyond the rooftops. The ringing was starting again when he opened the door. He found himself facing a young woman he had never seen before.

"The concierge did tell me . . ."

"What did the concierge tell you?"

"That you certainly wouldn't answer right away. It would be better if you gave me a key."

He still didn't understand. His head was splitting. He stared, confused, at the round little woman whose eyes had an expression that was far from being cold and who was just managing to keep from laughing.

"You can't have got to bed very early, can you?" she remarked.

She took off her thick blue wool coat. He didn't like to ask her who she was.

"Didn't the concierge tell you about me?"

He felt as if he hadn't seen the concierge for years.

"I'm the new cleaning woman. My name's Mina."

She put a parcel wrapped in tissue paper on the table.

"I gather I have to wake you at eight o'clock with a lot of coffee and croissants. Where's the kitchen?"

"It's only a kitchenette. In there."

"And the vacuum cleaner?"

"In the closet."

"Shall I wake you at eight anyway?"

"I don't know. No. I'll call you."

There was a ring of Brussels in her accent, and he almost asked her if she was Flemish. It was too complicated to do that then.

"Just as you like."

He went back into the bedroom, shut the door, frowned as he looked at the red hair, and put that problem to one side until later. He needed two aspirins urgently. He chewed them, because his doctor had told him that the membranes of the mouth absorb medicines more quickly than those of the stomach. He drank the water straight from the faucet.

He saw his pajamas hanging behind the door and took off his dressing gown so that he could put them on.

He couldn't remember anything. That had happened to

him only two or three times before in his life. The bath was full of soapy water. Had he been the one to take a bath? Or had it been the redhead?

He had had dinner with that idiot Blanchet. It had been dismal! It had been sinister! Had he slammed the door when he left? No. He could picture himself on the sidewalk with Fage. A really good man, he was. He would have liked to tell a man like Fage everything he had on his mind.

Of course he had things on his mind. People imagined that he never worried about anything because he habitually put on a cynical front. It would have been just the same even if Fage hadn't been his father-in-law.

He could picture him again, walking away in his long gray coat, down the street into the darkness.

He had had a drink. Not far away, in a café he didn't know, the first one he had come to. A café not at all like those he usually frequented. It was full of regulars. Civil servants, probably, playing cards. They stared at him. That didn't matter to him. They must have recognized him from his photographs, which had been in all the papers.

"A double!"

"A double what?"

"What are you, a fool?"

The proprietor was not impressed.

"If you want me to choose any bottle at random . . ."

"Whisky."

"You could have said so in the first place. Soda?"

"Did I say soda?"

He was feeling aggressive. He needed to let off steam.

"Plain water."

"Have you ever seen plain water before?"

He wasn't impressing anybody here.

"Plain, ordinary water."

One glass hadn't been enough for him. He had drunk three or four, and everyone was watching him when he made his way to the door.

He turned around to stare back at them. All idiots. The same type as Blanchet, but several grades lower. He had stuck out his tongue at them. After that he had taken some time to find his car again. The red one, of course. The yellow one was Kitten's. It was in the garage. His wife wouldn't be needing it for a long time.

It was odd, almost indecent, to think of his wife and his sister-in-law as children, then as adolescents. Where had he crossed the Seine? He could remember a bridge, and the moon showing through two clouds, and its reflection on the water.

He had needed to find some friends. He knew all the places where there was a chance of running into some of them. It didn't matter who. There wasn't a man in the world who had more friends than he.

He shouldn't have married. Either one chooses to have a wife, or . . .

"Nobody here?"

"I haven't seen anyone, Monsieur Alain. A double?"

"Yes, please, chum."

Why not? He had nothing else to do. They didn't need him at the office. Boris was doing everything. An odd fellow, Boris. All the people he knew were odd.

" 'By, Paul."

"Good night, Monsieur Alain."

That must have been Chez Germaine, on Rue Ponthieu. Then . . .

He took a third aspirin, brushed his teeth and gargled,

because his mouth tasted foul. He splashed cold water over his face and ran a comb through his hair. He didn't look particularly handsome. The sight of himself made him feel rather sick.

He had stopped off at other places, but where? They had all disappeared that night. Not one of the crowd to be found. What did that mean? Had they done it on purpose, so as not to meet him? Were they afraid to be seen with him?

He went back into the bedroom, picked up a bra and a pair of briefs from the carpet, and laid them on a chair. Then he pulled back the covers.

He found a face he had never seen before, a very young face, looking very innocent in sleep. The lips were pouted like a little girl's.

Who was she? What had happened?

Hesitating, he wondered if he should go back to bed and to sleep. He felt the veins in his eyes throbbing, and it was a very unpleasant sensation.

He went back into the studio, where the cleaning woman was beginning to clear up. She had changed out of her dress into a fairly transparent nylon smock through which he could see the black of her garter belt.

"What's your name?"

"Mina. I've told you that already."

She still looked as if she wanted to burst out laughing. It must have been a habit of hers.

"Well, Mina, make me some strong coffee."

"I should think you need some."

He wasn't annoyed. He watched her going toward the kitchen, swaying her hips, and he thought that one day sooner or later he would make love to her. He hadn't made love to a cleaning woman before. They had all been too old and he could only remember hard, tragic faces. Women who had had troubles and who bore a grudge against the whole world.

The yellow line in the sky had grown wider. The yellow had become brighter. It wasn't raining. He could see farther than on the last couple of mornings, as far as the towers of Notre-Dame.

Who should be telephoning him? That was one of the few thoughts to come to the surface: someone ought to phone him. It was important. He had said that he would be at home.

The familiar smell of coffee reached him. Mina wouldn't know that he took it in the big blue cup that he had had so much trouble getting, a cup holding three times as much as an ordinary cup.

He went toward the kitchenette. He saw from the look she gave him that she thought he was coming for another reason. She wasn't afraid. She was waiting, her back to him.

He opened the cupboard.

"This is my cup, the one I have every morning."

"Very good, monsieur."

Why was she always holding back a laugh? What had she been told about him? Someone must have said something to her about him. Thousands, tens of thousands of people were talking about him these days.

"I'll bring it right in to you."

She found him stubbing out a cigarette. The tobacco tasted terrible.

"You didn't have much sleep last night!"

He shook his head.

"I suppose the lady is still asleep?"

"How do you know there's anyone in my room?"

She went to a corner and picked up an orange satin shoe, very pointed, with a very high heel.

"There must be two of these, mustn't there?"

"That seems a reasonable assumption.",

She laughed.

"It's so funny."

"What's so funny?"

"Nothing. Everything. You."

He burned his mouth trying to drink his coffee.

"How old are you?"

"Twenty-two."

"Have you been in Paris long?"

"Only six months."

He didn't dare ask her what she had done during those six months. He was surprised that she had chosen to go out cleaning.

"Is it true that you only want me to come in the mornings?"

He shrugged his shoulders.

"It doesn't matter to me. What about you?"

"I'd prefer a full-time job."

"You can have it, then."

"Will you pay double?"

"If you want."

He was able to drink his coffee at last, in little sips. He was almost sick at the first taste, then his stomach got used to it.

"Won't the lady want any?"

"I haven't the slightest idea."

"Are you going to wake her?"

"Perhaps. I suppose I'd better."

"I'll make more coffee anyway. You only need to call."

He watched her walk away again, swinging her hips. Finally he pushed open the door, shut it behind him again, went up to the bed, and lifted the sheet up a few inches.

An eye opened. A blue-green eye. It looked at him from bottom to top, finishing with his face. She said in a worried voice, not moving:

"Hello, Alain."

She remembered. If she had been drunk, she hadn't been as drunk as he had.

"What's the time?"

"I don't know. It's of no importance."

Both her eyes were open now. She threw the sheet off, exposing two firm breasts, their pink tips hardly formed.

"How do you feel?" she asked.

"Terrible!"

"Serves you right."

She spoke with a trace of English accent, and he asked:

"Are you English?"

"My mother is."

"What's your name?"

"Don't you remember my name? Bessie."

"Where did we meet?"

He sat down on the edge of the bed.

"Is there any coffee about, just by chance?"

He found it hard to get up, to get to the studio, then to the kitchen.

"Mina, you were right. She wants some coffee."

"I'll bring it to her in a minute. No croissants? The concierge told me to bring some up."

"Yes, if you have any."

He went back to the bedroom. Bessie was no longer in the rumpled bed. He watched her come back from the bathroom, quite naked, and she got back into bed, pulling the covers up only as far as her knees.

"Whose is the toothbrush to the left of the mirror?"

"If it's green, it's my wife's."

"The one who . . ."

"Yes, the one who . . ."

There was a knock at the door. Bessie didn't move. Mina came in, holding a tray.

"Where shall I put it?"

"Give it to me."

The two women looked at each other, their curiosity free from embarrassment.

When the cleaning woman had gone out of the room, Bessie asked:

"Has she been here long?"

"Just since this morning. I saw her for the first time when I went to open the door for her."

She drank her coffee in great gulps.

"What was it you wanted to know?"

"Where we met."

"At the Grelot."

"On Rue Notre-Dame-de-Lorette? That's odd. I never go there."

"You were looking for someone."

"Who?"

"You didn't say. You kept saying it was a matter of life and death for you to find him."

"Are you a dance hostess?"

"A dancer. I wasn't alone."

"Who was with you?"

"Two of your friends. One was called Bob. . . ."

"Demarie?"

"I think that was it. He's a writer."

That was Demarie, who had won the Renaudot two years before, and who now worked for *Toi.*

"Who was the other one?"

"Wait a minute. A photographer—unhealthy-looking and sad. His head is a bit crooked."

"Julien Bour?"

"That's quite likely."

"With his clothes all wrinkled?"

"That's right."

Bour's clothes were always wrinkled and, possibly because he always tilted his head to one side, his face looked as if it had been stuck on crooked.

An odd man. He was the man who did the best photographs for the magazine. Not on-coming nudes such as one finds in other magazines. *Toi* was supposed to enter into people's private lives. Young girls should see themselves in it, and older women. A picture, for example, of a girl asleep with only one breast uncovered, a breast that took on a kind of universal meaning. Anyway, that was the sort of blah Alain served up to his staff.

"The text must look like a letter written by any one of our readers."

No sophisticated décors. A bedroom like most bedrooms. No faces that were too made-up, with long lashes, and scarlet lips parted over sparkling teeth.

The idea had come to him one afternoon while he was watching his sister-in-law dress. He had been writing articles at the time, mainly about the theater and cabarets. He had sold a few songs.

The title had come to him at once.

"*Toi* . . ." he had murmured under his breath.

"What about me? What makes me any different from other women?"

Exactly. She was just like other women.

"I have an idea. A new magazine. I'll tell you about it next time."

He had made a dummy, writing all the text himself. He hadn't known Bour then, and he had had great difficulty getting the press photographers he wanted.

"No, man. She doesn't look like a nice young girl."

"Can you see me asking a nice young girl for permission to photograph her bottom?"

A printer had given him credit. Lusin, who was now his publicity agent, had found the apartment on the fifth floor on Rue de Marignan.

"What are you thinking about?" the girl asked, nibbling a croissant.

"Do you think I'm in any state to be thinking? What was I doing in that place?"

"You talked a lot about a man who was the best man in the world."

"Didn't I say who?"

"You had just had dinner with him."

"My father-in-law?"

"Very likely. You wanted to tell him important things. Everything was important. You made me sit next to you and you slapped my thigh."

"Weren't the others annoyed?"

"The photographer wasn't very pleased. At one point you knocked over your glass. He accused you of having had too much to drink, and you threatened to push his face in. You also shouted an insult at him, one I'd never heard before. You called him a lump of glue! I really thought you were going to have a fight. The poor man did too, but he went away."

"Alone?"

"The other man had left us a few minutes before."

"What did we do then?"

"You ordered a magnum of champagne and said that it was foul stuff but it was a day for drinking champagne. You drank almost all of it. I only had two or three glasses."

"Were you drunk too?"

"A little bit. Quite a lot, maybe."

"Did I drive home?"

"The manager of the club wouldn't let you. You argued on the sidewalk for a long time and in the end you got a taxi."

He took the tray away from her, as she had finished with it.

"Did we make love?"

"Don't you remember?"

"No."

"I was half asleep and you were very angry. You shouted:

" 'Enjoy it! Go on and enjoy it, you bitch!'

"Then you slapped me a couple of times, still shouting the same words."

She laughed and looked at him with twinkling eyes.

"The funny thing is, it worked."

"Who took a bath?"

"Both of us."

"Together?"

"You insisted. Then you went and had another drink. Aren't you sleepy?"

"My head's spinning. I ache all over."

"Take an aspirin."

"I've already had three."

"Have you had your phone call?"

"No. I don't even know what phone call it is."

"You mentioned it at least ten times, and you frowned whenever you spoke of it."

He stroked her hip mechanically.

It was the first time any woman other than Kitten had slept in that bed. She had been there herself three nights before. What day was it?

Perhaps he shouldn't have . . . He would think about that later. His eyelids were burning.

He went back to bed. He felt better like that and he could hear the faint drone of the vacuum cleaner from the next room. His hand reached out for Bessie's thigh. She had the same soft, clear skin as Adrienne.

He didn't want to think of his wife, or of his sister-in-law. Twice, three times, he thought he had fallen asleep, but each time he realized he was only dozing. The world might be fuzzy and strange, there was still a world. There was even the rumbling of a bus in the distance, and sometimes a screech of tires.

He twisted around to pull off his pajamas and pushed them farther down under the bedclothes.

He could feel her warm body against his. He didn't move. He refused to pull himself out of the limbo he had sunk into, and it was she, with her pointed fingernails, who made the movements necessary for him to plunge himself into her.

This time he recognized the ringing of the telephone for what it was, and he woke up immediately. As he reached for the receiver he glanced at the clock. It was eleven o'clock.

"Hello. Alain Poitaud here."

"This is Rabut. I tried your office first. I'm still at La Petite Roquette. I'm going home, and I'd like to see you there in half an hour."

"Is there any more news?"

"That depends on what you mean by news. I need you."

"I'll be there. I may be a little late."

"Don't be too late. I have another appointment and I have to be in court at two."

He got out of bed and took a shower. He was still there when Bessie came into the bathroom.

He put on a terry-cloth robe and began to shave.

"Will you be out for long?"

"I haven't the slightest idea. I might be out all day."

"What about me? What shall I do?"

"Anything you like."

"Can I go back to bed for a little?"

"If you want."

"Don't you want to find me here when you come back this evening?"

"No. Not this evening."

"When?"

"We'll see. Leave your telephone number. Do you want money?"

"I didn't come for that."

"I'm not asking you why you came. It's all the same to me. Do you need money?"

"No."

"Right. Go and pour me a whisky. You'll find a sort of bar in the studio."

"I saw it last night. Can I go in there the way I am?"

He shrugged his shoulders. Five minutes later he put his trousers on. He added a little water to the whisky, which he drank at a gulp, as if it were a medicine. He remembered that his car wasn't at the door. He would have to go and get it later, from Rue Notre-Dame-de-Lorette.

"I'm sorry, chum. It's business."

"I know that. Whom are you going to see?"

"The lawyer."

"The lawyer who'll defend your wife?"

He went into the studio.

"Well, are you going to have me for the whole day?"

"That'll be fine. You'll find a key on the kitchen table. That'll be yours. Wake me tomorrow at eight o'clock with coffee and croissants."

He went down the stairs three or four steps at a time and stopped a taxi at the corner of the street.

"Boulevard Saint-Germain. I think it's number 116."

He was right. He remembered that Rabut's apartment was on the third floor, and he took the elevator. He rang the bell. A bespectacled secretary opened the door and seemed to recognize him.

"Come this way. I'm afraid you'll have to wait a moment. Maître Rabut is on the telephone."

There was a double door on the right, and on the left a corridor with offices opening onto it. One could hear the clacking of typewriters. Rabut employed several qualified young lawyers doing their three years' probation, and they came into the corridor one after another to take a look at Alain.

The door opened at last.

"Come in. I've just spent an hour with your wife."

"Has she decided to speak?"

"Not in the way we had hoped. She's keeping silent on that subject. And on other matters too. But she didn't throw me out, which is always something. Did you know that she is a very intelligent woman?"

"I've often been told so."

He did not add that that wasn't the quality he admired most in a woman.

"She has a strength of character such as is rarely found. This is her second day in prison. She has been given a little cell to herself. They wanted to put her in with another prisoner, but she refused. She may change her mind."

"Is she wearing a uniform?"

"Before they are tried, the prisoners wear their own clothes. She doesn't have to work. There's no question of getting her to say that you may go and see her. She is adamant on that point. She doesn't shout or get excited. One can tell, when she says anything, that it's useless to press the matter.

" 'Tell him that I shall not see him again, except at the trial, and that only because it is required and we shall be kept far apart.'

"Those are her own words. When I told her how upset you are, she calmly replied:

" 'He has never needed me. He needs people, any people. It doesn't matter to him who is at his side.' "

This phrase struck Alain with such force that he heard no more of what followed.

"He needs people."

That was true. He had always needed to be surrounded by people he called his chums, or by his colleagues. Left on his own, he became nervous, with a strange, morbid nervousness. He didn't feel safe, and that was why, although he had been drunk, he had brought a girl home the night before. What would he do that evening? And the next day?

He imagined himself sitting alone in the former studio, gazing at the spectacle of Paris by night.

"Her father will see her this afternoon. She agreed right away to seeing him.

" 'Poor Father! It's he who will find this hardest to take.'

"When I told her her mother was ill, she wasn't concerned, she wasn't even interested.

"I wanted to talk to her about her defense. We can't let her get a sentence of twenty years, let alone a life sentence, and so we need a motive that will influence the jury. I can only see that a *crime passionnel* will do. You don't enter into it."

"Why?"

"You told me the reason yourself. It's almost a year since you've seen her sister. It would be difficult for me to plead delayed jealousy. Don't think that the police aren't doing anything. If they haven't already done so, they'll find the room where you used to meet, before this evening. We must find the other man."

He glanced at Alain, who had turned pale.

"Is that absolutely necessary?"

"I thought I had already said that. I'm not saying that it will be pleasant for you, but it's a fact, unless we've all got hold of the wrong end of the stick. Haven't you noticed any difference in your wife's behavior these last months?"

Alain had grown pale; now he felt his face was reddening, because he had suddenly made a discovery. He hadn't followed his thoughts through as far as this until now. It had taken Rabut's brutal question to reawaken his memories. . . . That and perhaps what had happened in bed with Bessie that morning.

For years Kitten had always been eager in their sexual

relations. They had often played a little game which was a secret between them. She would be reading, watching television, or writing an article. He would murmur suddenly:

"Look at me, Kitten."

She would turn toward him automatically, then burst out laughing.

"That's it! Right! I can't concentrate any more. What do you have that acts on me in such a way?"

But several times since the beginning of the summer she had said, annoyed:

"Not today, do you mind? I don't know what's wrong with me. I feel tired."

"That's not like you."

"Maybe I'm getting old."

Rabut was watching him.

"Well?"

"Maybe."

"Unpleasant or not, you must reveal all that to the public at the trial. You want her to be acquitted, don't you?"

"Of course."

"Even if she doesn't want to come back to you?"

"From what she's said to you, she doesn't mean to go on living with me whatever happens."

"Do you still love her?"

"I suppose so."

"The police have been thinking about it. Maybe they'll find our man. In my opinion you are in a better position to do so, since the chances are it's someone you know."

Rabut realized that the other man was looking a bit sick.

"What's the matter?"

"Nothing to worry about. Last night I had to have dinner

with my brother-in-law. Afterward I had too much to drink. I'm still listening to you."

"She said one more thing which struck me and which I forbade her to say to anyone else. I was talking to her about your son Patrick. I asked her to think of him and of his future. At that point she remarked, almost dryly:

" 'I've never had any maternal feelings.'

"Is that true?"

Alain was forced to reflect, to remember instances in the past. When Patrick was born they hadn't been well off. It was just before the idea of the magazine had occurred to him. Kitten was very busy with the baby, taking care of it with a meticulousness that was sometimes a bit exaggerated. Exaggerated in the same way as, when typing one of her articles, she would begin a page again when she found a typing error.

They had lived together in Paris, the three of them, for almost two years. Then they had engaged a nurse, and from that moment on Kitten had launched herself again into her work, meeting him anywhere and coming home when he did, late at night.

It didn't even occur to her to go and look at the sleeping child before she went to bed. Most times, Alain did that alone.

They had bought Les Nonnettes and rebuilt it, and they went there every weekend. She used it mostly as a place in which to work.

"I know what she means," he murmured.

Rabut stood up and looked at the clock on the wall. A bell on his desk rang. He picked up the telephone receiver.

"Yes. Put the call through. He's still here."

And, holding the phone out to Alain, he said:

"It's your office."

"Hello, is that you, Alain? Boris here. I've been trying to get hold of you for the last half hour. I phoned your apartment, and a woman whose voice I didn't recognize said you'd rushed out after getting an urgent phone call. She said something about a lawyer. I phoned Helbig, and he wasn't in. When I got him he said you would be with Rabut.

"There have been new developments here, within the last hour. Superintendent Roumagne arrived with two of his men. He showed me a paper signed by the magistrate, and he took over your office. He went through everything in the drawers. Then he asked me for a list of the staff. He told me he wanted to see everyone but that it wouldn't take long. He has decided to begin with the switchboard girls."

"I'll be right over."

He hung up and turned to Rabut, who was growing impatient.

"Superintendent Roumagne is in my office with two other policemen. He has gone through my drawers and he's questioning my staff. He has decided to begin with the switchboard girls."

"What did I tell you?"

"Do you think he suspects one of my colleagues?"

"Whatever he thinks, he's there, fishing for clues, and you won't be able to stop him. Thank you for coming. Try to find out who our man is."

Our man! The phrase was so ironic that Alain could not hold back a smile.

"You need a drink. You'll find a little bar on the left as you go out."

Alain felt annoyed with Rabut. He was annoyed with him

about everything, about the way he had summoned him to his office, the way he had repeated Kitten's words, the way he had put his finger on Alain's need to drink.

He waited for the elevator, his head bowed, and found himself indeed at the counter of the little bar.

"A double scotch."

"What?"

"A double whisky, then."

Some workmen in overalls looked at him curiously. He had no desire to meet Roumagne. He too would guess, just by looking at him, how he had spent the night.

He wasn't ashamed. He was a free man. He had devoted his life to thumbing his nose at people, and to scandalizing them, on purpose.

Why should he suddenly feel upset when people stared at him? He hadn't done anything. He had had nothing to do with what had happened. Thousands of husbands sleep with their sisters-in-law, that's a well-known fact. Younger sisters tend to want to steal what belongs to their elder sisters.

Adrienne had never loved him, and he hadn't given a damn. Maybe Kitten had never loved him either?

And anyway, what did that word mean? Love—he sold a million copies of it every week. Love and sex. It came to the same thing.

He didn't like to feel that he was alone. Not because he wanted intellectual conversation, not even because he needed affection.

"Rue Notre-Dame-de-Lorette!" he called to the driver as he slammed the taxi door shut.

What did he need? Someone to be there, in fact, anyone at all. Old people living by themselves have a dog, a cat, a canary. Some are happy with just a goldfish.

He had never thought of Kitten as a goldfish, but, thinking things over with a fresh eye, he realized that for him she had been, above all, someone who was there. Someone at his right side, a few inches from his elbow.

He waited for her phone call in the mornings and in the afternoons, and he grew nervous if it was late. How many times, in seven years, had they had a real conversation?

At the time he was starting the magazine he had talked to her, of course. He was completely absorbed in it, sure it would be a success. She used to smile indulgently at him.

"What do you think of it?"

"It's already completed, isn't it?"

"That's not the same thing. You don't seem to understand the personal aspect, the intimate side. Today we try to personalize everything, just because everything is mass-produced, even our leisure activities."

"Maybe that's true."

"Will you join the team?"

"No."

"Why?"

"The boss's wife shouldn't be one of the staff."

And there had been Les Nonnettes, too. They had discovered the house one Saturday afternoon when they were driving around in the country. That Sunday, at the inn where they had stopped, he was already making plans.

"We need a house in the country, don't you see?"

"Perhaps. Isn't it a bit far from Paris?"

"Far enough not to have people we don't want dropping in on us all the time. Not too far to put our friends off."

"Do you expect to ask many?"

She didn't object, she let him do what he liked, she fell

in with his plans. But she didn't share his enthusiasms.

"Stop here, driver, behind that red car."

"Is it yours?"

"Yes."

"I think I can see two or three parking tickets on the windshield."

The driver was right. He had had two summonses. The key was still in the dashboard. The engine took some time to start. He looked at the night club he had never been in until the previous night. He recognized Bessie's picture among photographs of nude girls. It was in the middle, and bigger than the others, indicating that she was the star attraction.

He got to Rue de Marignan and drove his car into the courtyard. He hesitated before going upstairs. It was after twelve o'clock. The rooms on the ground floor were shut.

Had he reached the stage where he was afraid of a deputy superintendent of the Criminal Police?

He got into the elevator. The corridors and most of the offices were empty. The door of his own office was wide open, and he found Boris waiting there for him.

"Have they gone?"

"About ten minutes ago."

"Did they find out anything?"

"They didn't say anything to me. Are you hungry?"

Alain made a face.

"You look like a corpse."

"I have a hangover, that's all. I'll try to eat something with you, and you can tell me what happened."

He had expected to find his desk in a mess. It wasn't.

"Your secretary put everything back in its place."

"What was he like?"

"The superintendent? Polite. There was a pile of photographs on the desk, ones I had turned down because they were too daring. He took a good ten minutes to go through them. He's just a dirty old man, like everyone else!"

Chapter Six

THEY found a restaurant where they weren't known, near Place Saint-Augustin, a mock bistrot with red-checked table-cloths and curtains, and quantities of brass ornaments. The proprietor was dressed as a chef, in a tall white hat, and went from table to table telling the customers what they should eat.

They got a table in a corner, even though the place was crowded. All these people eating and talking were complete strangers to Alain. He knew nothing about them. They had their own lives, their own problems, their own little universes in which they revolved quite seriously as if they had an important function to fulfill.

Why were all these people necessary to him? For example, it wouldn't have entered his head to have lunch alone in his apartment with Boris. He could have planned his life another way.

They had tried to at one time, he and Kitten. She had taken it into her head to do the cooking. They would eat, seated facing each other, in front of the wide bay window through which they would look at the Paris skyline.

After a while like that, Alain would look at his wife's moving lips. He knew that she was talking, but her words weren't getting through to him, or, if they were, they didn't make sense. He had the feeling that they were cut off from life, that they were trapped, motionless, in an artificial world from which, panic-stricken, he was trying to escape.

This wasn't just a bad dream he had. He needed to move, to hear noise around him, to see human beings coming and going, to be surrounded.

Surrounded, that was it. Did he need to be the center of things, the chief character?

He wasn't yet able to admit that. He had always had friends around him, and maybe it was because of his fear of finding himself alone that he dragged the evenings' entertainments on until late at night.

Friends? Or were they really a group of courtiers he had got together to build up his self-confidence?

They took a selection of hors d'oeuvres from a trolley, and he forced himself to eat, washing it down with great gulps of vin rosé.

"What did he ask *you*?"

"More or less the same as he asked everyone else. First of all, if your wife often came to see you or to get you at the office. I said no, she used to telephone and we would meet her downstairs or in a restaurant. Then they asked if I knew your sister-in-law. I told them the truth. I've never seen her."

"She came once, three years ago. She wanted to see the place where I spend most of my time."

"I was away. Then he asked me if you didn't have a notebook with personal telephone numbers. Do you have one?"

"No."

"That's what I told him. He asked one more question. I must apologize for repeating it. He asked if I knew that your wife had a lover. Could I imagine any one of your colleagues who might be this lover? Can *you* think of anyone?"

In a voice stripped of all illusion, he answered:

"It could be anyone."

"Then he called the switchboard operators in. Maud was the first one to come up. You know what she's like. He let me stay there during all the interrogations. Maybe he did it just so that I could tell you what went on at them. Maud's went something like this:

" 'How long have you worked for Monsieur Poitaud?'

" 'It'll be four years next month.'

" 'Are you married?'

" 'I'm single, I have no children, and I don't live with a lover but with an old aunt who's as nice as can be.'

" 'Are you one of Monsieur Poitaud's mistresses?'

" 'If you mean do I sleep with Alain, yes. From time to time.'

" 'Where?'

" 'Here.'

" 'When?'

" 'When he feels like it. He asks me to stay on after hours. I wait until everyone has gone and then come up.'

" 'Does that seem natural to you?'

" 'It certainly isn't unnatural.'

" 'Has no one ever walked in on you?'

" 'No, never.'

" 'What would you have done if his wife had come in?'

" 'I expect we'd have gone on.'

" 'Do you know Adrienne Blanchet?'

" 'I just know her voice.'

" 'Did she phone often?'

“ ‘About two or three times a week. I put her through to the chief. They never talked for long.’

“ ‘When was the last time she telephoned?’

“ ‘Last year, before the Christmas holiday.’

“ ‘Did you know that Alain Poitaud was having an affair with his sister-in-law?’

“ ‘Yes. I used to telephone Rue de Longchamp.’

“ ‘Did he ask you to phone?’

“ ‘To book the room and to have a bottle of champagne chilling. She must have liked champagne. He didn’t.’

“ ‘Has this not happened since last December?’

“ ‘Not even once.’

“ ‘Did she never try to reach him?’

“ ‘Never.’ ”

Boris was eating hungrily, while Alain felt sick at the sight of the food on the plates.

“The other two switchboard girls confirmed what she had said about your sister-in-law. Then it was Colette’s turn.”

His secretary. The only one who seemed a bit jealous.

“When he asked her if she slept with you she started off by twitching and talking about one’s private affairs being secret. She ended up by admitting it.”

She was thirty-five and treated him as if he were a baby. She would have loved to cuddle him all day.

“The stenographers and the girls in Accounts were all seen, too, and then the men.

“ ‘Married? Children? Give me your address, please. Did you often have dinner with the chief and his wife?’

“I signaled to them that they should tell the truth. He asked them too if they knew your sister-in-law. Then he wanted to know if they had ever met Kitten alone.

"Some of them were finished with very quickly, Diacre, for example, and Manoque."

Diacre was as ugly as sin, and Manoque was sixty-eight.

"Bour was the last one to come in. He had just got to the office and he looked nearly as badly hung over as you."

"We spent some time together last night. With Bob Demarie. We were all tight."

"That's all. I got the impression that the superintendent is no fool and that he knows exactly what he's after."

Before the steak they had ordered arrived, Alain lit a cigarette. He didn't feel well, mentally or physically. The sky was a bilious color. So was he.

"It is Friday, isn't it?"

"Yes."

"They've got the body laid out in the apartment on Rue de l'Université. I wonder if I should look in."

"You'll know that better than I do. Don't forget that it was your wife who . . ."

He didn't finish the sentence. Of course, Alain thought, it was his wife who had killed the person who was lying in the coffin.

He went back to the office. If he hadn't had to drive Boris back, he might well have gone home to sleep.

"Maître Rabut's secretary asked if you would telephone as soon as you came in."

"Put me through."

A few moments later Colette held the receiver out to him.

"Monsieur Poitaud? This is Maître Rabut's secretary."

"I know."

"Maître Rabut apologizes for having forgotten to phone you this morning. Your wife has sent him a list of things she would like you to take her as soon as possible. Shall I send it to you?"

"Is it very long?"

"No, not very."

"Then dictate it to me."

He pulled a pad of paper toward him and wrote the list of things she wanted, one below the other.

"First, a gray jersey dress that is in the left-hand wardrobe unless she has sent it to the cleaner's. She thinks you'll know about that. A black wool skirt, the newest one, with three big buttons on it. Four or five white blouses, the plainest ones. It takes a week to get one's washing done in that place."

He felt he could see Kitten, hear her, even. It was the same nonsense every time they went to a hotel.

"Two white nylon slips—the ones without any lace. About a dozen pairs of stockings, the newest—they're in a red silk case."

She was in La Petite Roquette, accused of murder. She might well get a life sentence and she was worrying about things like stockings.

"Are you sure I'm not going too fast for you? Black patent-leather slippers, and her slippers for the bath. Her bathrobe. A pair of black flat-heeled shoes. A bottle of her usual perfume, just a small one. You'll know which it is."

Even her perfume. She wasn't in the least worried! She was all right, she had both feet planted firmly on the ground!

"A few sleeping pills and her indigestion tablets. Oh, I was forgetting. She also wants her brush and comb."

"Did she write the list herself?"

"Yes. She gave it to Rabut, asking him to get it to you as soon as possible. She has added a word I can't read very well. It's written in pencil, on terrible paper. So . . . Yes, it is two r's. *Sorry*."

They had the habit of talking and writing to each other in English. Sorry! *Excusez-moi.*

He looked at Colette, who was watching him, thanked Rabut's secretary, and hung up.

"I hope you weren't too upset by your interrogation."

And, since she opened her eyes in astonishment:

"I'm sorry. I called you *vous*. Did it upset you to have to confess that we sleep together sometimes?"

"It's nobody's business."

"That's what one thinks. Everyone thinks his private life belongs to him alone. Then something happens and everything is laid open to the public gaze."

He added, in a voice full of irony:

"*I* am being laid open!"

"Does it hurt?"

"No."

"Isn't that just a pose?"

"I swear to you that those two women could have slept with every man in the world without its upsetting me in the least."

Poor Colette! She was still sentimental. She might have been one of *Toi*'s readers. She must have been one of the few among the staff to take the magazine seriously.

She would have preferred to see him prostrated with grief. He would have put his head on her shoulders and she would have comforted him.

"I'm off. I must take her her things."

He got into his car again, in the courtyard, and once more followed the route he knew so well. The air was getting fresher. The passers-by were walking more cheerfully than the previous evening and even doing a little window-shopping.

He took the elevator, let himself into the apartment, and was surprised at first to find the new cleaning woman there. She must have decided to work full-time, then. The wardrobes and drawers in the hall were open.

"What are you doing, chum?"

He was still calling her *vous*. He was surprised at himself. It wouldn't last.

"If I'm to be of use to you, I have to know where everything is. At the same time, I'm brushing the clothes that need brushing."

"In that case, you can give me a hand."

He took the list out of his pocket and went to look for a large suitcase.

"The gray jersey dress."

"It needs to be sent to the cleaner's."

"My wife couldn't remember whether she had sent it or not. Too bad. Hand it over."

Then the slips, briefs, stockings, shoes, all the other things.

"Here, let me do it. You're just shoving them in any old how."

He watched her with some surprise. She wasn't only a pretty girl, young and attractive, she seemed to know her job, too.

"Are you taking them to the prison?"

"Yes."

"Even the perfume?"

"That's right. As long as they are only detained there, they have special privileges. I don't know just how free they are."

"Have you seen her?"

"She doesn't want to see me. By the way, the woman who was in my bed this morning . . ."

He listened to hear if Bessie was still there.

"She got up shortly after you left, asked me for some coffee, and came into the kitchen to help me get it ready."

"With no clothes on?"

"She had put on your dressing gown. It was lying on the floor. We talked for a bit. I ran a bath for her."

"What did she say?"

"She told me how you'd met, then what happened last night. She was a bit surprised that this was my first day here, and then she said that you would surely need me soon."

"What for?"

She replied calmly:

"For everything."

"Pour me a whisky—not too much."

"So early?"

He shrugged his shoulders.

"One gets used to it."

"Are you often the way you were last night?"

"Almost never. I drink, yes, but I'm hardly ever drunk. This morning was only the third or fourth hangover I've had in my life. Hurry up."

That was it. He was calling her *tu*. One more chum. He needed to draw people into his circle, and that circle was situated a little, maybe quite a lot, below his level.

Was that the way it really was? He had never thought about it. He had believed that his friends were a group of people who liked the same things and whom he could count on.

That wasn't true. Many other things he had believed to be true, weren't. One day he would make a list, like Kitten with her clothes, her underwear, her shoes, and all the rest.

He wondered if his brother-in-law was at his office in Place Vendôme in spite of the body's being laid out. It wasn't very likely. He was probably standing stiffly, dressed in black, at the door of the drawing room, near the coffin and the flickering candles.

"Hello, Albert? May I speak to my brother-in-law? Yes, I know. I only want to say something to him very quickly."

A procession interrupted, as might be expected. Great numbers of dignitaries, deputies, perhaps a Minister or two. The Blanchets held a high position in the hierarchy. Who could tell how far they might go?

Why was he sneering? He wasn't jealous of them. He had no desire at all to be like them. He couldn't stand them. Besides, he despised them for all the things they did to keep up appearances. In a word, a word it gave him great pleasure to use, they stank.

"It's me, Alain. I'm sorry to interrupt you."

"This is a long, unhappy day for me, and . . ."

"Quite. That's what I wanted to speak to you about. I suppose there must be reporters and photographers all around your house."

"The police are trying to keep them away."

"I think it would be better if I didn't show up."

"I agree."

"As for tomorrow . . ."

"You must on no account come to the funeral."

"I was going to say that. I am the husband of the murderess, isn't that it? Not to mention . . ."

What was getting into him?

"Is that all you have to say?" Blanchet interrupted.

"That's all. I am truly sorry. It has nothing to do with me. The police are of that opinion too, now."

"What have you been telling them this time?"

"Nothing. The superintendent questioned my staff. Then they went to Rue de Longchamp."

"Won't you give me any details?"

"You have my sympathy, Roland. Tell my father-in-law that I'm sorry I won't see him again. He's a good man. If he should need me for anything, he knows where he can reach me."

Blanchet hung up without waiting to hear any more.

"Was that the husband?"

"My brother-in-law, yes."

She gave him an almost mocking look.

"What do you find so funny?"

"Nothing. Do you want me to get a taxi and take the suitcase?"

He hesitated.

"No. I'd better go myself."

It would be a contact, in spite of everything. It wasn't really love, not what people usually mean by love. Kitten had trotted at his side for years. She had been there.

What exactly had she said to Rabut? That she would never see him again except at the trial, and then only at a distance.

And what if she were acquitted? Rabut had the reputation of getting nine out of ten of his clients acquitted.

He imagined the president of the court, the magistrates, the advocate-general, then the jurors coming in in single file, looking self-important, and their foreman reading out:

". . . to the first question: no . . . to the second question: no . . ."

The murmuring in the room, perhaps some protests, some whistling, journalists crowding against each other, running to the public telephones.

What would happen then? What would she do, standing between two guards, wearing a plain dark dress or a suit?

Rabut would turn around to shake her hand. Would she look for Alain among the crowd? Would he stay there to look at her?

Would she smile to someone else?

"Tell him I won't see him again, except . . ."

Where would she go? She wouldn't come home, where most of her belongings were still in their places. Would she come and get them? Or would she send him a list, as she had done that morning?

"What are you thinking?"

"Nothing, chum."

He patted her behind.

"You have a firm backside."

"Do you prefer them soft?"

He almost . . . No, not then. He had to go to Rue de la Roquette.

"See you later."

"Will you be back this afternoon?"

"Probably not."

"Then I'll see you tomorrow."

"Yes, tomorrow."

His expression grew serious. That meant that he would come in to the empty apartment, that he would be alone, that he would pour himself a last drink, looking at the lights of

Paris, and finally he would go into the bedroom and undress.

He looked at her again, nodded and repeated:

"See you tomorrow, chum."

He had handed the suitcase over to a matron whose manner was that of complete indifference, and now he was driving around a district he hardly knew at all. A few moments before, he had passed the Père Lachaise cemetery, where a few faded leaves still clung to the trees, and he had wondered if that was where Adrienne would be buried the next day.

The Blanchets must have a family vault somewhere, most likely a monument of marble in many colors. Alain had never called her Adrienne, but Baby. Wasn't she a part of his circus too?

In a few minutes Kitten would open the suitcase and, with a serious expression and a little frown, put away her clothes and her underwear.

She would be organized. Now she had her own private life. He couldn't imagine her cell. In fact he had no idea at all of what life was like in La Petite Roquette, and that annoyed him.

Would she be with her father? Would they be talking to each other through a grille, the way people did in films?

He found himself back in Place de la Bastille, and he went toward the Pont Henri IV so that he could drive along the banks of the Seine.

Friday. Only last Friday, like almost every Friday, he and his wife had been in the Jaguar, driving on the west-bound speedway. The minis were for Paris, for town driving. For longer trips they used the Jaguar convertible.

Would she be thinking about that, too? Wouldn't the dismal world around her, with its smell of disinfectant, depress her?

What good did it do to think of things like that? She had decided not to see him again. He hadn't flinched when Rabut had told him that. He hadn't even felt a cold shiver up his spine. That phrase meant so many things!

In fact, she must be feeling free, rather like a widow. She would find her own personality again. She wasn't tied any longer to someone whom she had to meet in this place or that as soon as he phoned.

She would be able to speak. It wouldn't be he who did all the talking, the person everyone listened to, but she. Already she was a separate person in the eyes of the lawyer, of the magistrate, of the warders, of the head of the prison—she was a person in her own right.

When he left the speedway he only had to drive through a wood and he could see Les Nonnettes standing in the middle of the fields. Last Christmas they had bought a goat for Patrick.

The boy spent almost all his time with the gardener, Ferdinand—a fine man—and with Mademoiselle Jacques, his nurse. That was her surname. Patrick called her "Mammy," which had annoyed Kitten at first. She was "Mummy." But, in the child's estimation, Mammy was the more important.

"Tell me, Daddy, why don't we all live here together?"

Yes, why hadn't they? He shouldn't have thought of that. It didn't help and was a dangerous line to pursue. He would go to Les Nonnettes the next day.

"And where is Mummy? Where is she?"

What would he answer? Still, he must go. Besides, the offices in Rue de Marignan were closed on Saturdays.

He couldn't turn his car into the courtyard because a tank

truck was unloading oil. He parked as best he could and glanced at the queue of people at the little windows as he went in. As well as there being competitions, the competitors had organized a club. They even had badges.

It was all nonsense, of course. Starting with one floor and a few second-hand desks, he had managed to take over the whole building, and in a year it would be completely rebuilt. The magazine's circulation grew bigger month by month.

"Hello, Alain."

The old friends, the ones he had had around him from the first, those who were part of his circle when he was just a reporter, called him "Alain." The others called him "Chief."

"Hello, chum."

He liked to walk up the stairs, to go through the different departments, to go along the narrow corridors, to go up and down the steps, surprising his colleagues at their work.

He wouldn't look annoyed when he found a group of five or six in one office, telling stories and roaring with laughter. He would laugh with them. Not today.

He climbed steadily upward, trying to free himself from the confusion of thoughts that were crowding in on him, little niggling thoughts, annoying, like certain dreams. Some of them were so vague that he couldn't have put a name to them, but their combined force was crushing him.

It was a bit like having doubts about everything. Or being at his own autopsy.

He found Maleski in his office.

"No, mademoiselle," he was saying into the telephone, "we know absolutely nothing. I am terribly sorry. I have nothing to say."

"Still about . . . ?"

"Of course. Now we're getting them from the provinces.

That woman was calling up from La Roche-sur-Yon. I have a message for you. Superintendent Roumagne phoned. He wants you to go to his office as soon as you can."

"I'll go there now."

After all, it didn't inconvenience him. He didn't know what to do with himself anyway. He was sure that he was in everyone's way.

Before going to see the superintendent he went into the bar across the street from the office for a double whisky. As he had said to Mina, he wouldn't overdo it. He only drank out of habit.

He had always drunk like that, maybe because he needed to live one degree above reality. His friends drank too. Except the ones who left the group after they got married and only met the others from time to time. With those, the woman had won. Doesn't the woman always win, even though she doesn't seem to?

When all was said and done, hadn't Kitten won, too?

Mina had entered the apartment for the first time at seven that morning. By eleven or eleven thirty she had already managed to make it a full-time job. God only knew if he wouldn't find her waiting there in the evening. It probably wouldn't be long before she was spending her nights on Rue de Chazelles.

"A double?"

Why ask? He wasn't ashamed of drinking, of being almost an alcoholic. It wasn't a vice any more these days, but an illness. He couldn't help it if he was ill.

"Not too busy just now?"

People are very good at putting their foot in it. The bartender, who had known him for years, hadn't meant to say anything wrong.

"I'm up to here with . . . !"

"I'm sorry. I thought . . . Another drink?"

"No."

He didn't pay. He settled his account at the end of the month, like most of his colleagues who went down to have a drink from time to time. At first they used to take bottles up to their offices. It didn't take them long to see that that wasn't the same thing, that they were drinking mechanically, just pouring it down.

What could the deputy superintendent want with him? Why wasn't it the magistrate who wanted to see him?

He could hide at a street corner the next day, to see the funeral procession going past. . . . She used to have a funny way of looking at him. . . . He could still see the mocking light in her eyes that she had always refused to explain. . . .

"What are you laughing at, Baby?"

"You."

"Why? Am I so funny?"

"No."

"Does my face make you laugh?"

"Of course not. You're quite good-looking."

Quite . . .

"Is it when I speak?"

"It's everything about you. You're a dear."

Well, he didn't like to be called a dear, even though he called others chums, babies, or little ones.

Was she the only person, in fact, who didn't take him seriously? For the others took him seriously, the printers, the messenger boys, the banks. No one thought of him as a little boy, or as a clown.

"Have you an appointment?"

A policeman stopped him at the door of the Criminal Police.

"Superintendent Roumagne is waiting for me."

"The stair on the right."

"I know."

He didn't meet anyone on his way up. The usher on the next floor made him fill in a form. He put a question mark in the space marked "Reason for visit."

He was not kept waiting, and the inspector who was with Roumagne when Alain was shown in disappeared immediately.

This time the superintendent shook hands with him and had him sit in an armchair.

"I wasn't expecting you so soon. I wondered if you would be going in to your office at all. I know you usually go to the country on Fridays."

"That's already a thing of the past," he replied ironically.

"Do you feel bitter?"

"No. Not even that."

The superintendent looked like a countryman. His grandfather or his great-grandfather would still have been a peasant. He was thick-set, a big-boned man. He looked straight in front of him.

"I suppose you have nothing new to tell me, Monsieur Poitaud?"

"I don't know what might be of interest to you. Do you want to know that I spent the night getting drunk? That I woke up this morning with a terrible hangover, *plus* a tart in my bed?"

"I know all that."

"Are you having me followed?"

"Why should I? It wasn't you who shot your sister-in-law, was it?"

His voice grew harder.

"I hope you weren't annoyed that I took over your office this morning and took the liberty of going through your drawers."

"That doesn't matter."

"I questioned your staff."

"Now it's my turn to say I know that."

"It confirmed what you told me yesterday about your relationship with your sister-in-law."

"Which was?"

"That that relationship finished before Christmas last year. The person who rents the room in Rue de Longchamp is quite sure on that point."

"I hadn't any reason to lie to you."

"You might have had."

The superintendent was silent. He lit a cigarette and pushed the pack over to his visitor, who took one out of habit. Alain realized that this silence was intentional. He pretended to find it quite natural, and he went on smoking and looking at nothing.

"I want you to be quite honest in your answer to the question I am going to ask you. You must realize its importance. What would your reaction be if I were to tell you who your wife's lover was?"

"You mean my wife's and my sister-in-law's lover?"

"That's right."

Alain clenched his fists for a second. His expression grew hard. It was his turn to let a silence grow.

"I don't know," he said finally. "It would depend."

"On who the man was?"

"Possibly."

"If, for example, it was one of your colleagues?"

In a flash he imagined the whole building in Rue de Marignan from top to bottom and called to mind the faces of the young men and the not-so-young, even the old ones, eliminating them one by one. François Lusin, the publicity manager, a dandy who thought himself irresistible to women? No! Not Kitten, anyway.

Not Maleski either, or little Gagnon, his editorial secretary, with his birdlike movements and his childlike plumpness.

"Don't try to guess. I'll tell you in a minute."

"Do you know, then?"

"I have means at my disposal that you don't have, Monsieur Poitaud. Because of this I find myself in a delicate situation, and that is why I have asked you to come here. You will have noted that I didn't order you to come. This is in no way an official interview. How do you feel?"

"Terrible," he answered in a hard voice.

"I'm not concerned with your hangover, but with your nerves."

"If that's what you want to know, I'm as calm as the poison someone's just drunk."

"I wish you would take this seriously. I know Maître Rabut well enough to know that he will plead a *crime passionnel.* If he is to do that, he needs a third person to fit the bill."

"I can see that."

"You won't do, since you broke off your relationship with your sister-in-law almost a year ago. It will be a lot more than a year ago when the case comes up at the assizes."

He bowed his head. He was calm, in fact. Deadly calm.

"Your wife refuses to talk. She still has the right to a fair trial, and if it can be proved to be a *crime passionnel* . . ."

"Cut out the drivel, won't you? Make it quick, please."

"I'm sorry, Monsieur Poitaud, but I must be sure that I don't provoke another incident."

"Are you afraid I'll kill him?"

"Your reactions are fairly violent."

He laughed, bitterly.

"On whose account would I kill him? On my wife's? I'm getting used to the idea that I've lost her. I've thought about it a lot. I knew that she was there, and that was enough for me. Now that she isn't there any longer . . ."

He gesticulated vaguely.

"As for Baby, I mean Adrienne . . ."

"I understand. You have your pride. You are a proud man, and I admit you have cause to be pleased with yourself."

"I'm not."

"You're not pleased with yourself?"

"No."

"Don't you care at all who took your place with the two sisters?"

"I don't think so."

"Do you have another gun?"

"I only had that Browning."

"Will you promise not to get one?"

"I promise."

"I believe you. Now wait for a surprise. My men went to question the concierges of the buildings where some of your colleagues live, the ones who seemed most likely. Usually it's the last call that's the right one. This time it was the first, as luck would have it. The nearest address, on Rue Montmartre."

Alain wondered which of the men in his offices lived on Rue Montmartre.

"Julien Bour."

The photographer with the twisted head and the ugly face! The man he had met the night before on Rue Notre-Dame-de-Lorette!

"Does that surprise you?"

He gave a forced smile.

"I find it a curious choice."

Bour was the last man he would have thought of. He wasn't particularly concerned with "personal daintiness," and it was very likely that he never cleaned his teeth. He didn't look people in the eyes, as if he were afraid of them.

In fact, Alain knew hardly anything about his past. Before joining *Toi* he hadn't worked for any of the important weeklies or for any of the big dailies.

Who had introduced him to Alain? He searched his memory. It had been several years before. It wasn't anyone connected with the magazine, and it had taken place in a bar.

"Alex!" he said aloud.

"I was wondering how I had met him. It was a man called Alexandre Manoque who told me about him. Manoque is some kind of film producer in a vague sort of way. He's always talking about films he's going to produce, but all he's ever done are two shorts. On the other hand, he knows an incredible number of pretty girls, and we give him a ring when we're short of models."

He couldn't get over it. Filthy old Bour! Bour, a man not

one of the secretaries would have looked at. They said he smelled, but Alain, at least, had never noticed it.

He hardly ever went out with the crowd, and when he did he was just like an extra on a movie set. Everyone would have been stunned if he had joined in the conversation.

He brought his photographs and climbed up to the attic to arrange the make-up with Léon Agnard, for he was a meticulous workman.

"Both women!" Alain whispered, shattered.

"Except this time it was in reverse."

"What do you mean?"

"Your wife was the first one to start going to Rue Montmartre."

"She went to his apartment?"

"Yes. It's an enormous building, almost falling down, mainly offices and workshops. There's the photographic studio, for example."

"I know it."

A weekly gossip magazine that he had worked on at the beginning of his career had had its offices there. There were enameled plaques on almost all the doors. Rubber Stamps. Photocopying. Hubert Moinat, Expert Translator. E.P.C. Agency.

He had never found out what the E.P.C. Agency was, since the weekly had run for only three issues.

"He has a big room and two smaller ones right at the top, looking out on the inner court. He uses the big room as a studio and does most of his photography there. My inspector showed the concierge the photographs of your wife, and she recognized them at once."

"Such an elegant lady! So nice!" she had exclaimed.

"When did it start?"

"Almost two years ago."

Alain had to stand up. He couldn't understand it. Kitten had been in love with Julien Bour for two years and he hadn't noticed a thing! She had gone on living with him. They had made love. They had slept naked in the same bed. It had just been over the past few months that she had grown less passionate.

"Almost two years!"

He started to laugh, a hard, cruel laugh.

"And her sister? When did that dirty rat seduce her sister?"

"Only three or four months ago."

"Did each one have her special day?"

The superintendent was watching him calmly.

"At the end it was Adrienne who went there more often."

"To get even with her sister, by God! It was her turn at last!"

He paced about as he would have done in his own office or in the studio in Rue de Chazelles.

"Does my brother-in-law know about this?"

"It isn't the time to tell him. Isn't tomorrow the day of the funeral?"

"Of course. I understand."

"Besides, it's not for me to tell him. . . . If Maître Rabut thinks it's better to inform him . . ."

"You've told *him*, then."

"Yes."

"Was he the one who told you to tell me to come here?"

"I would have done that anyway. There are reporters following every possible trail. They had got to Rue de Longchamp before we did, and one weekly paper of the type you were just talking about mentions it today."

"Bour isn't even the kind of man you can punch in the face," Alain grumbled.

"I know a few more things about him. His name seemed familiar to me. I went to see my opposite number in the Vice Squad, and he has been interested in Bour for several years."

"Has he a record?"

"No. No proof. A few minutes ago you mentioned a name: Alex Manoque. I can tell you that his real name is spelled with a *ck*: Manock. The Vice Squad has had its eye on him for a long time—some business about dirty photos. Manock has been shadowed. He often met Julien Bour, always in cafés or bars. Bour was certainly the one who took the pictures, but a search of his apartment on Rue Montmartre didn't bring any films to light.

"I don't know if they're still in that line. It's not my business and it has no bearing on our case. My colleague is sure it isn't only stills, but movies too."

"Do you think he photographed my wife?"

"I don't think so, Monsieur Poitaud. My first idea was to go and see him and look over his files of photographs. But that could stir up a lot of trouble just now. We don't often manage to do things unobserved, especially when every reporter in the place is on our tail."

"Bour!" Alain said again, looking at the floor.

"If you'd been in my job for twenty years you wouldn't be so surprised. Women often need someone weaker than they are themselves, or someone they think is weaker than they are, a man who arouses their pity."

"I know the theory," Alain said, impatiently.

"You may be sure it's true in practice."

Alain understood that much better than the superintendent did, and that was why he had grown so melancholy.

He knew enough now. He was in a hurry to get away.

"Will you promise me . . ."

"Not to kill Bour? I won't even touch him. I doubt if I'll even sack him, since he's our best photographer. You see, you have nothing to worry about. Thank you for telling me. Rabut will get her acquitted. They'll live happily ever after and have lots of children."

He went toward the door, then stopped in his tracks, turned, and held his hand out to the superintendent.

"Excuse me. I forgot myself. I'll see you before long. You'll be bound to have something new to tell me."

He allowed himself the luxury of saying, as he passed the old usher with the silver chain:

"Good night, chum."

Chapter Seven

HE didn't stop by his office. He didn't have any desire to see "them." Maybe he wanted to prove to himself that he didn't need them, that he didn't need anyone. He sat at the wheel of his little red car and drove straight ahead until he found himself in the Bois de Boulogne, where he turned around and drove off again without any particular destination in mind.

He was just trying to pass the time, nothing else. He looked at the trees, at the dead leaves, at two men on horseback who were chatting together as they rode along.

He had learned too many unpleasant truths in too short a space of time, and he needed to digest them slowly.

He didn't feel any need to drink. He stopped at a bar he didn't know, near the Porte Dauphine, but that was only because he didn't want to change his habits too abruptly. He looked at the people around him who were drinking and wondered if they had the same problems he did.

Not quite the same. The thing that had just happened to him was fairly out of the ordinary. But the basic problems couldn't vary a great deal from man to man.

Other eyes were gazing into space, just as his were. What were they seeing? What were they looking at?

"I think I know you," murmured a fat, red-faced man sitting near him. He had had too much to drink already.

"You most certainly don't," Alain answered dryly.

He had decided how he would proceed that day, and he stuck to his decision. He dined alone, in a restaurant that was new to him, on Avenue des Ternes. It was a restaurant mainly frequented by regulars, and had a set of wooden pigeonholes for their napkins.

He wasn't hungry, but he ate anyway, soup first, followed by a grilled *andouillette* with French fried potatoes. The proprietor stared at him but kept his distance. It was a lucky thing that the photograph that had appeared in the newspapers didn't look very much like him.

Some people frowned, looked at him for a bit, then shrugged their shoulders, deciding that they must have been mistaken.

He went into a movie house on Champs-Elysées and sat where the usherette took him. He didn't know the title of the film. He recognized most of the American cast, but he couldn't follow the plot.

Remaining faithful to his plan, he lived through the rest of the day, hour by hour. Later on he went home. He went up in the elevator and let himself in.

The rooms were all empty and gloomy. Mina hadn't dared to stay. She must have thought of it, but she would have been afraid of acting too quickly.

He put on the lights. There was a tray on the table, with a bottle of whisky, a glass, and some soda water.

He sat down in an armchair, poured himself a drink, and felt more remote from his fellow men than he had ever felt before in his life. His reactions had been almost the same when he had failed his examinations. He remembered that. He imagined himself back on the balcony of their apartment on Place Clichy, watching the streets spring to life as night fell.

Did those little black figures wandering around on the pavements really know where they were going? He had almost gone back into his room and written a poem about it.

His sense of the ridiculous had come out on top. He had looked for the paths that were open to him and hadn't found any that satisfied him.

How many times, when he was a child or a teen-ager, had he been asked:

"What are you going to do when you grow up?"

As if he had any say in that! From his earliest years he had had the impression that his future would depend on chance, on a meeting, on something he happened to hear. He wouldn't be pushed about, that was one sure thing. He wouldn't get stuck, like his father, in a narrow corridor where he would waste his life struggling on only to find that there was nothing at the end of it.

He could remember every detail. His parents, in the dining room, must have been talking about him, because they were whispering. They didn't want to hurt him by reminding him of his failure.

"You'll pass when you come up again in October."

Two cars had crashed in the square below, and a small crowd had gathered around. The little ants gesticulated. It was both sad and grotesque.

There was only one solution, one only, which he didn't like but which he accepted since there was nothing else. He would join the army.

There was complete silence around him in the apartment on Rue de Chazelles, and he jumped when some woodwork in the studio creaked.

He didn't have to go out again, any more than he had had to leave his balcony in Place Clichy before being sure that he had made the right decision.

"Aren't you coming in?" his father had come to ask him.

"No."

"Aren't you cold?"

"No."

"Good night, my boy."

"Good night."

Then his mother had come to say good night to him. She hadn't pressed him to come in. His parents were both a little afraid, since they knew he was sensitive, that a wrong move on their part might turn him into a rebel.

He hadn't rebelled. He had been a soldier, like everyone else. It had been rather like a retreat for a Christian. It had been a time of preparation. He had learned to drink, one evening a week only, since he had only enough money for that.

He gave the bottle an ironic glance. It seemed to be thumbing its nose at him, defying him. It was enough for him to put his hand out toward it, a gesture so familiar that he could have done it without even noticing.

He stood up to look at the skyline, at the silhouette of Notre-Dame outlined against a fairly clear sky, at the dome of the Panthéon.

To hell with them all!

He went into the bedroom, looked at the empty bed, and began to undress. He wasn't sleepy. He didn't want anything. There was no reason why he should be here rather than anywhere else. Pure chance. Kitten had been chance, too. And Adrienne, whom he had nicknamed Baby. Why did he have this thing about nicknaming people?

"Hell!" he said, aloud.

He said it again as he was standing in front of the bathroom mirror, brushing his teeth.

Bour must be afraid, waiting for him to come. Who could tell? Maybe he had bought a gun, to defend himself. Maybe he had left Paris suddenly.

He gave an ironic smile, put his pajamas on, and put out the lights without going near the bottle of whisky.

"Good night, pal."

He had to say good night to himself because there was no one else to say it to him.

He did not go to sleep right away. He spent the time lying motionless in the dark, pursued by unpleasant thoughts. In spite of that, he must have gone to sleep rather quickly because the sound of the vacuum cleaner in the studio came as a surprise to him.

He realized that he had had a disturbed night when he saw the tangled sheets. He couldn't remember anything he had dreamed, although he had dreamed a lot.

He got up and went into the bathroom, brushed his teeth, and ran a comb through his hair. Then he went into the studio. Mina switched the vacuum cleaner off.

"Up already? Did I wake you?"

"No."

"I'll get your coffee right away."

He watched her as she went. His fingers weren't trembling the way they had done the previous evening. He didn't have a headache. Only a sort of empty feeling, and not too unpleasant at that.

It was as if he wasn't concerned with things any more, as if all responsibility had been removed from his shoulders.

What responsibility, in fact? How could one man be responsible for another man's actions, or for a woman's, or even for a child's?

Bugger!

A word he didn't usually use. It was new to him. He rather liked it. He tried it out two or three times, looking at the pale, early-morning sun.

Mina brought him his coffee and croissants.

"Did you get home late?"

"No, chum."

She glanced toward the bedroom.

"Is there anyone there?"

"There's no one here but ourselves."

He ran a coldly appraising look over her figure. It must be impossible to tell what he was thinking, he thought. He felt that he was beyond normal, everyday thoughts.

"Do you want to see the paper?"

"No."

She stood above him, arching her back, making her breasts stick out farther. She was only wearing her briefs and bra under her nylon smock.

He thought it over, weighing up the pros and cons. At first she had given him an encouraging smile, then a blush of embarrassment flooded her young pink cheeks.

He didn't eat any croissants, but finished his coffee and lit a cigarette. He held the pack out to her, then lit her cigarette.

She smiled again. He stood up and looked her up and down once or twice. Then he looked her straight in the eyes, a questioning look. She understood at once, just as a bartender understands that he should refill the glasses.

She laughed. There was no need for an answer.

"Do you want me to undress?"

"It doesn't matter."

She put her cigarette in the ashtray, pulled her smock over her head, and lifted first one foot and then the other to take her briefs off. Her pubis was fair and well-rounded, and her stomach still had its adolescent fullness.

"Why are you looking at me like that?"

"Like what?"

"You look sad."

"I'm not."

She had taken off her bra. She was quite naked. She was a little overawed by him and didn't quite know what to do next.

"Come here," he said softly, after stubbing out his cigarette.

He had said it softly, gently.

"Lie down . . ."

It was as if he were putting her to bed to sleep. He didn't look at her with desire in his eyes, but more as if he wanted to fix the picture of her body in his memory.

"Aren't you . . . aren't you going to lie down too?"

He took his pajamas off and lay down beside her, running his hand over her skin.

She was surprised. In her experience, things didn't happen like that. He seemed so different from the man she had seen the day before.

"Was it a long time ago, the first time you made love?"

"I was fourteen."

"Was he young?"
"It was my uncle."
She laughed.
"That's funny, isn't it?"
He didn't laugh.
"When was the last time?"
"Three weeks ago."
He pulled her to him and kissed her, a long, tender kiss that was not meant especially for her. It wasn't meant for Kitten either, or for Adrienne, or for any woman in particular.
"Are you sad?" she asked again.
"I've already said no."
"You look sad. I thought . . ."
"What did you think?"
He smiled at her.
"I don't know. Nothing. Kiss me again. I've hardly ever been kissed like that."
Her skin was very clear. He had never seen a woman with such a clear skin. She was soft, too. He kissed her. He caressed her with his hand while his mind remained far away.
He took her once, slowly and tenderly. He didn't recognize himself any more, either. He stroked her from head to foot, with his hands and with his lips, and she hardly dared to believe what was happening to her.
They lay clinging together for a long time. When he looked at her at last he saw the same question in her eyes, a question he could not answer.
When eventually he got up, the first thing he did was to turn his head away.
"Are you crying?"

"No."

"I don't expect you cry very often, do you? I'm sorry if you don't like my saying *tu*. In a few minutes, when I put my smock on, I'll call you *vous* again. Do you mind?"

"No."

"May I use the bathroom?"

"Of course."

She was just going to shut the door when he came in. A little surprised, she let him watch her, anyway. It was a different kind of intimacy, other movements common to all women.

"You know, that's the first time that . . ."

She hesitated, still a little overawed. It seemed to her that he was both very close to her and, at the same time, very far away.

"That what?"

"That it's been like that. So . . . so gently . . ."

He went into the shower and stood still, the water pouring over him.

"May I take a shower too?"

"If you like."

He put on his dressing gown and went to pour himself a scotch. He sipped it slowly, gazing at the view from the window. For him, it was over. He wasn't even thinking about it any more. She was a part of the past. That was what she couldn't understand.

Who could understand? Not even he! Not really.

"It's funny," she said, coming back into the studio to dress. "Men are usually sad after they've made love. I always feel gay, light-headed. I want to sing, to turn somersaults."

"What do you mean, turn somersaults?"

"As when I was a little girl."

She put her head on the floor, threw her legs in the air and turned over several times.

"Haven't you ever done that?"

"Yes."

It didn't bring back any childhood memories to him. Quite the contrary.

"Would you fasten it?" she asked him, holding the back of her bra to him.

The same gesture as Kitten's, as all the others'. What do women do when they're on their own?

"Thank you."

He poured himself another small whisky, which he drank in one gulp, lit a cigarette, and went to the closet in the hall. He chose a pair of gray flannel trousers, a tweed jacket, soft shoes with crepe soles. He took off his dressing gown and put on a polo-necked sweater.

"You're going to look very sporty."

He didn't react. He didn't react to anything, now.

"Aren't you going to put on a coat? It's sunny, but it isn't warm."

He took down a suède jacket and looked all around him. He saw her at last, when he was almost at the door. She stood on tiptoe, reaching for his lips.

"Don't you want to kiss me?"

He hesitated.

"Yes."

He gave her the kind of kiss he would have given a sister.

"Will you be back before evening?" She had started to call him *vous* again.

"Maybe."

He went downstairs slowly, stopping twice. He could hear

children's voices on the second floor. He almost pushed open the glass door of the concierge's quarters, but he had nothing to say to her and he wasn't interested in any letters there might be.

He got into the car and drove to his garage on Rue de Courcelles.

"Good morning, Monsieur Alain. Are you taking the Jaguar?"

"Have you filled her up?"

"She's all ready, oil, battery, everything. Do you want me to put the top down for you?"

"Yes, please."

He got behind the wheel and drove toward Saint-Cloud, through the tunnel and out onto the west-bound speedway. There was no one in the seat beside him, no one to tell him not to drive too fast.

It was funny to think that Kitten would be organizing her own little life in La Petite Roquette.

He drove so slowly that many other cars passed him and people turned around to stare at him. It was unusual to see a sports Jaguar dawdling along the road.

He was in no hurry. His watch told him that it was a quarter past eleven. He looked at the trees as though he had never seen them before in his life. Some of them had red leaves, some golden yellow, and others yet were dark green. Sometimes he caught sight of a dirt road, a real dirt road with ruts in it. He hadn't been on a road like that for years.

Some meadows, a farm with black and white cows standing around. In the background, a line of mist that clearly marked the winding course of the Seine.

There was a breeze, but he wasn't cold. Several trucks passed him. He had once been a truck driver, in the army, in Africa. In fact, he had done a good many things in his life.

He almost forgot to take the turn-off to the right to go under the speedway to Les Nonnettes. Kitten usually had to remind him. There were hardly any other cars on the road.

When he saw the slate roof and the little square turret, he realized that he hadn't had a cigarette since leaving Paris. He could see Ferdinand's battered old hat over the top of a low wall. Patrick would be somewhere near, in the kitchen garden.

He went through the gateway—the gates were kept open all day—and parked the car in the driveway, in front of a small flight of stone steps. Mademoiselle Jacques, wearing a blue uniform she must have designed herself, opened the door.

"I wasn't sure if you would be coming. Patrick is in the kitchen garden."

"I guessed he would be when I saw Ferdinand. He doesn't know anything, does he?"

"No. I warned all the people who came to the house. There's only the postman and the tradesmen."

He looked at the white house with its little square windows, the house that had given him so much anxiety. It had been a sort of dream come true for him: the house he would have liked to be born in, or the house where he might have spent holidays with his grandparents.

The huge kitchen had a red tiled floor. All the other floors were well waxed. The walls of the big, rustic living room were white, to look as if they had been whitewashed.

"You look tired."

"I'm less tired than I was yesterday."

"It must have been a terrible shock."

"Yes, it was, terrible."

"Were you by yourself?"

He nodded.

"How is your brother-in-law?"

"He took it better than I would ever have believed."

He walked toward the kitchen garden, its low walls covered with neatly espaliered fruit trees. There were enormous pears, already turning yellow, and apples on which Ferdinand lavished his love, tying them up in bags to keep the insects off as soon as the fruit began to swell.

The paths were neat, the vegetable beds marked off with string, not a weed in sight.

Patrick and the gardener were busy picking string beans when the child saw Alain. He ran toward him and jumped into his arms.

"You're early. Where's Mummy?"

He was looking around to see if he could see her.

"She had to stay in Paris."

"Won't she be coming tomorrow?"

"I don't think so. She has a lot of work to do."

Patrick didn't seem too upset. Ferdinand had taken off his filthy old hat, and his bald white head gleamed in the sunlight. Since his face was weathered by the sun, browned over and over again, the ivory color of his scalp looked almost indecent.

"Nice to see you, Monsieur Alain."

"Mummy didn't come, Ferdinand. She has too much to do. You won't forget you promised to make me a bow and arrow, will you?"

The gardener could have posed as a model for a child's picture book. The house was a picture-book house, too.

"Are you coming, Patrick? It's almost time for lunch."

For there was even a gong, by the kitchen door, and Loulou, Ferdinand's wife, always rang it for meals.

"Hello, Loulou."

He could smell rabbit cooking, with little onions and herbs.

"Hello, Monsieur Alain."

She could only stare fixedly at him, for she didn't dare ask him any questions in front of the child.

"Mummy won't be coming," the boy announced.

Whom did he look like? He had his mother's eyes, brown, lively, and dreamy at the same time, very alert, but the lower part of his face was more like Alain's.

Loulou, under her checked apron, was plump with dumpy legs. Her gray hair was twisted into a hard little bun on top of her head.

"Lunch will be ready in a few minutes. Will you have some fillets of herring? Patrick asked for them."

He didn't hear her. He went past the dining room and into the living room, where there was an antique cabinet in which they kept the drinks and glasses.

He poured himself a whisky. His son watched him gulp it with interest.

"Is it good?"

"No."

"Better than lemonade?"

"No."

"Then why do you drink it?"

"Because it's a thing grownups do. Grownups don't always know why they do what they do."

Mademoiselle Jacques threw him a warning look and he realized that he would have to watch what he said.

"Will there be people coming tomorrow?"

"No."
"Nobody?"
"Nobody at all."
"Can we play together, just the two of us?"
"I won't be here either."
"When are you going away?"
"Very soon."
"Why?"
Yes, why? How could he tell a five-year-old boy that he couldn't stand more than two or three hours of the atmosphere of Les Nonnettes and what it stood for?
The nurse was surprised too. The maid, coming down the stairs, asked:
"Are there any bags to take up?"
"No, Olga."
The gong rang. A wasp buzzed by. He had forgotten that there were wasps.
There were only three of them seated around the oval table in the dining room. There was a big bunch of flowers in a blue pottery vase on the table.
"Aren't you having any herring?"
"Yes. I'm sorry."
"What's wrong? You look tired."
"I am tired. I've been working hard."
That was true. Terrible work. Work one does only once in one's life. He had gone right down to the very depths of himself. He had scratched the surface, then stripped the layers off until he bled. It was over. He couldn't bleed any more. But he could never be the same man again.
Mina hadn't understood that she had had what was undoubtedly a unique experience that morning.
Neither Patrick, nor the nurse, nor anyone here could

understand any better than she had understood. He went on eating. He smiled at his son.

"May I have a little wine in my water, Mammy?"

"Tomorrow. You only have it on Sundays."

"Daddy won't be here tomorrow."

She looked at Alain and poured a few drops of red wine into the child's glass.

It was an interminable meal. The window was open. They could hear the birds singing, and flies came into the room from time to time and flew around the table before flying out into the sunshine again.

"Will you take your coffee in the drawing room?"

They called it the drawing room, or the hall. He went in there and sat down in one of the brown leather armchairs. The hood of the Jaguar was in the sun, but he didn't have the energy to get up and move it to another place.

"I'm going to see if Ferdinand has finished his lunch. He promised he'd make me a bow and arrow."

Mademoiselle Jacques didn't know whether she should go or stay.

"Have you any instructions for me?"

He thought for a long time.

"No. Better not."

"Is it all right if I go and see what Patrick's doing?"

He finished his coffee, went toward the stairs, and did a tour of inspection of the bedrooms. They were low-ceilinged. The furniture was almost farm furniture, heavy peasant pieces, but together they looked bright and natural.

It was a studied naturalness. A false naturalness. A naturalness calculated to charm the weekend guests.

Just as *Toi* had created a false intimacy.

Just as . . .

It was no use! It was too late. Or too soon. He opened the door of his bedroom and looked at it without any emotion.

He went downstairs and saw his son standing with the gardener, who was making a bow and arrow for him. Mademoiselle Jacques was standing some yards away.

What good was there in hanging about? He joined them and bent over Patrick and kissed him.

"Will you be back with Mummy next weekend?"

"Maybe."

He was more interested in the bow than in his father.

Alain shook the nurse by the hand.

"Are you leaving already, Monsieur Alain?"

"I have to, Ferdinand."

"Do you need anything? Wouldn't you like to take some fruit back to Paris?"

"No. Thank you just the same."

He went to say good-by to Loulou, who began to cry at once.

"Who would have thought that this would happen, Monsieur Alain!"

She wiped her eyes with a corner of her apron.

"Someone so . . ."

So, so . . . what? He left the house in a daze, raced the engine, and left Les Nonnettes in a cloud of dust.

Chapter Eight

Now he could drink, and he had to. Everything he had done that day, even the smallest detail of what had happened with Mina, had been foreseen, planned in advance. Wasn't it odd that the role had fallen to a little Flemish girl whom he hadn't known two days before and who had appeared at his door as if by a miracle!

Not an important role, maybe, certainly not more important than Mina thought.

He was ahead of schedule. He had spent less time at Les Nonnettes than he had thought he would, as he had felt stifled there. His departure, which he would have liked to be calm and serene, had looked like a flight.

He drove quickly, heading away from Paris. It didn't take him long to get to Evreux, a place he had often driven through. He looked for a bar and only saw bistrots with yellow- or mauve-washed walls that certainly wouldn't serve whisky.

He got lost in a tangle of roads which all looked alike, and that took up a few minutes. Finally he found a sign pointing to Chartres.

Why not Chartres? He had driven for only about a quarter of an hour when he found a tourist-type inn with an old carriage on the lawn for a sign. There would certainly be a bar there.

There was one, and a bartender listening to the racing commentary.

"A double!"

He was going to explain, but the bartender had understood and grabbed the bottle of Johnny Walker. He wasn't the only man to order his drink with that phrase. A double scotch. A double whisky. A double. These were the only words that made him feel any better.

"A good day for a drive."

He answered vaguely that it was. He didn't care what the weather was like. That had nothing to do with his program. It wasn't a parade.

"Another double."

"I've seen you in here before, haven't I?"

Of course, chum. Everyone had seen him. Even people in places he'd never been. Just because his picture had been on the front pages of the papers.

"Good-by."

"See you again."

Other people must be envying him his car. He shot down a road that wasn't meant for that sort of thing. He had to turn around again, taking a lot more than a three-point turn to do it.

Chartres! Here he was. He had seen the cathedral windows before. He particularly remembered a restaurant with a pleasant bar, at a street corner. He found it.

"A double scotch."

Things were going all right now. He was getting into gear, finding his rhythm bit by bit. This time he lost the little game with the bartender.

"You were here two years ago, weren't you?"

"No, monsieur. I came here last month."

"Well, where were you before that?"

"In Lugano."

Alain had never been to Lugano. Wrong! He could be wrong sometimes too, couldn't he?

He drove on, looking at the cars driving in the opposite direction. Their drivers had such serious expressions.

All his life he had been just the opposite of serious, and people had believed that that was how he really was. They had seen him so gay and extroverted that no one had guessed that he was just a little boy dressed up as an Indian.

In fact, he was just as afraid as the others. Even to the extent of hardly daring to look them in the face. Those were the times when he called them "chum" or "little one."

It had worked. They had left him alone. But had it really reassured him?

He hadn't had enough to drink. In a few minutes, when he went through Saint-Cloud, he would stop again. There was a big place where there was dancing on Saturday evenings. He had been there one Saturday with one of the typists. That was the time when Kitten had gone to Amsterdam to interview someone. An American professor, if he remembered rightly.

They had made love on the grass, by the banks of the Seine.

No one had exposed that trick of his, either. He wasn't afraid of women, not really afraid, but they overawed him.

It all stemmed from his childhood, from the first books he had read. He tended to put women on a pedestal.

So he lifted up their skirts and took them. No more pedestal.

He found himself on a spur of the west-bound speedway and went in to Saint-Cloud. He remembered to stop at the dance hall. The décor had changed. So had the atmosphere. Still, there was a bar.

"A double scotch."

Things weren't going as quickly as they had gone two nights before. He was still quite calm, remembering the warning Superintendent Roumagne had given him. He had promised. A good man, the superintendent. He had understood a lot, almost too much. Wouldn't Alain have liked to be a man like that?

A man one could rely on. A man who didn't need to . . .

What the hell! It was too late.

"How much was that?"

That was one more task done. The night before it had seemed very important to him to make this trip. He had planned the program and he wasn't going to change it.

Some ridiculous thoughts, like that last one about the superintendent, kept popping up suddenly in his mind. Things seemed far off, people were fuzzy in his mind, and he could hardly remember what they looked like.

The Champs-Elysées. He looked down Rue de Marignan, gazed at the façade of the building where a huge TOI was lit up every night.

He parked his car on Place de la Bourse and stopped in a journalists' bistrot. He sometimes used to have a boiled egg there, in the old days.

"A glass of red wine, please."

The waiter in his blue apron was too young to remember him, and yet it wasn't very long ago.

"Another one."

Two swift glasses of red wine. That hadn't been on the program. He was trying to keep to it meticulously.

"How much?"

He didn't blame either of them. Kitten had followed him as best she could. Perhaps she had believed in him. Perhaps she had thought he needed her. It didn't matter now.

She had had enough of being Kitten, of living in his shadow. She too had wanted to play the leading role.

The leading role! That was funny.

He went into the old building on Rue Montmartre as if he were going home and began to climb the worn steps, littered with cigarette ends. The walls hadn't been repainted, and the enamel plaques were still on the doors.

On the door where the sheet he had once worked for had had its office there was a sign:

ADA

Artificial Flowers

Was this a new way of disguising a brothel? "Ada" gave him food for thought. Maybe they did funeral wreaths too. Washable? In plastic?

Two floors more. He was hot. He went along a corridor. There wasn't a plaque on the third door on the right, but a visiting card covered with cellophane.

JULIEN BOUR

ART PHOTOGRAPHER

Art photographer! That was all! The key was in the door. He opened it and found himself in a big room with spotlights all over the place. There was a red light on over a door. A voice called.

"Don't come in. I'll be right out."

It was Bour's voice. What was he expecting? Had the superintendent warned him Alain would be coming?

In a corner a box mattress, mounted on four wooden blocks and covered with a Moroccan rug, served as a divan and as a bed. Alain opened another door, which led into a tiny bathroom with a footbath. There were yellow streaks, from years of dripping, under the faucets.

He closed the door, turned around and found Bour standing in front of him. He was in his shirt sleeves, with no tie. He was rigid, almost corpselike.

"Bour, chum."

Bour looked toward the door as if he wanted to run.

"Sit down. Don't worry. I'm not going to do anything to you."

Why had he thought this visit so essential last night? Seeing poor Bour so scared, so pitiable, hadn't any effect on him. Nor did seeing the divan where Kitten and Baby had rolled around, each in turn. Even trying to imagine Bour naked didn't move him.

"I swear, Chief . . ."

"What the hell does it matter, my God! I just wanted to look at you, that's all. I am looking at you. Maybe you're right not to take too much pride in your appearance. Some women must go for that."

He lit a cigarette and went over to look out into the courtyard, which was filled with ten handcarts, or thereabouts. This must be one of the last remaining yards in Paris where one would find handcarts instead of cars.

"Are you expecting anyone?"

"There'll be a model coming in."

Alain stared at him. It's a funny thing to stare at a man from whom you don't expect anything, a man about whom you aren't even trying to form an opinion. It's as if you were staring at an animal. You watch him breathing. You look at his frightened eyes. You notice his trembling lip and the beads of sweat springing up under his nose.

"Wouldn't you like to take my photograph?"

That hadn't been on the program either. It was just an idea that had suddenly come into his head.

"Why? Do you really want . . ."

"Yes, really."

"A portrait?"

"Why not?"

Bour got up and walked uncertainly over to one of the spots and switched it on. He went to look for a camera on a tripod that was standing in a corner. He must have expected to be shot or hit when his back was turned.

Alain didn't move.

"Full face?"

"Do it the way you think best."

Bour focused the camera. His fingers were trembling.

"Did you take any photographs of Kitten?"

"I swear I didn't."

"Why all this passion for swearing? Just say no and I'll believe you. Didn't you ever want to photograph her lying naked on the bed?"

"No."

"What about Adrienne?"

"Adrienne asked me to."

"Did you do it?"

"Yes."

"Do you still have the negatives?"

"No. She destroyed them. She only wanted to see what it felt like."

"In what pose?"

"Lots of different poses."

He heard a click.

"Hadn't you better take another one?"

"No, I'm sure that one's good."

"Have you any whisky?"

"No. There's only some wine left."

He looked at Bour once again, straight in the eye, their noses almost touching.

"Good-by."

What had he expected? What had the deputy superintendent been afraid of? Nothing had happened. He hadn't felt anything. When you got down to it, Bour wasn't important. He had only played his part by accident.

Where was his car? He looked for it in the street and remembered that he had left it on Place de la Bourse.

From now on he had plenty of time. What he needed was to find congenial bars. Preferably bars where nobody knew him. He didn't want to talk.

The most annoying thing was finding a parking place for his car every time. But he needed the car. He went up Rue du Faubourg-Montmartre, but he didn't want to drive through Place Clichy again. That was all in the past, as far as he was concerned, like Les Nonnettes. There was some logic in his ideas.

He found himself back at the Madeleine again. In a bar

with prostitutes patiently waiting. He wasn't looking for a woman.

"A double scotch."

The women kept giving him encouraging looks. He looked at them just as he had looked at Bour, as if they had been fish, or rabbits, or any other living, breathing animal. It's a strange thing to watch someone breathing.

"Another one, man."

It was hard to find bars where he wasn't known. He tried a new one on Boulevard Haussmann. The bartender was wearing a red jacket.

"A double."

"Johnny Walker?"

The drink was smooth. It had no taste.

"Am I beginning to look drunk?"

"No, monsieur."

It was true. He could tell that when he looked in the mirrow, but he had wanted confirmation of it. The back of the room was in shadow. There was a couple holding hands on a padded bench.

He had to believe that they were there. He shrugged his shoulders and almost forgot to pay. In fact, he had to be reminded.

"Good-by, Bob."

"My name's Johnny, monsieur."

"Good-by, little one."

He was still keeping up appearances, in spite of himself.

Just suppose . . . No! It was too late to change his mind now. He had had all the time in the world to think about it. But just suppose, just for curiosity's sake, that he were to go back into his office on Monday. . . . Right. . . .

Everyone would pretend. Boris would be the first of them. . . .

Only he, Alain, wouldn't be able to pretend any more. . . . That was it! Not with anyone . . . not even alone. . . .

It was chance, that's what it was. Kitten couldn't have known, when she'd fallen for Julien Bour, that one day she'd shoot her sister.

Now she knew that. And she had had Rabut tell him that he wouldn't see her again.

"Except at the trial."

He felt he must seem foolish, even more foolish than an article in *Toi*.

"A double, bartender."

"Martini, monsieur?"

"Scotch."

He was somewhere behind the Palais Bourbon, not far from his brother-in-law's. He wondered if Blanchet had looked at himself in a cold light yet. His brother-in-law wasn't so stupid. He would know how dangerous it could be.

As for beginning again . . . How? Beginning what?

If he hadn't failed his *baccalauréat*. It wasn't any good looking for excuses. He would have failed something else.

"Another."

The bartender looked at him for a second before serving him. That meant he was beginning to get drunk. It wouldn't be long now.

"Don't worry, I can hold it."

"Everyone says that, monsieur."

What was wrong with bartenders these days? They were always so solemn.

He emptied his glass. His steps, as he walked toward the door, were just too dignified to hide a certain unsteadiness. Sitting in the car, he had difficulty lighting his cigarette.

"He needs you, Alain."

That was his mother's voice. He thought he could hear her, could see the lifeless eyes of a woman who had never had any pleasure in all her life. Nor had his father.

How did he need his son? Not any more than his mother did, did he? They didn't need him, either of them.

Patrick would be better off with Mammy, as he called her, and with the old couple. He wouldn't know Les Nonnettes was a sham, a broken dream.

He would inherit a lot of money. The million readers, men and women, mostly women, had made Alain rich.

It wasn't fair. His father had worked all his life from morning to night to scrape a living, while Alain, joking one night with his friends, had discovered a gold mine.

Where was he? He didn't know where he was any more. The boulevard he was driving along seemed endless. He wanted to go toward the Bois de Boulogne and not toward the outer ring road.

He turned, heard a whistle, and stopped, sheepishly, afraid that the whistle might spoil everything.

"Don't you know that this is a one-way street?"

The policeman mustn't see that he was drunk.

"I'm sorry. How do I get to the Bois de Boulogne, please?"

"You're going away from it. Take the first turn to the right, then right again and straight on until you get to the Pont Alexandre III."

Whew! He had a right to have one last glass, not immediately, but when he got to the entrance to the Bois. He found himself on familiar ground and went into a café. He had a bad taste in his mouth.

"A whisky."

"Ordinary whisky or the good stuff?"

He pointed to the square bottle of Johnny Walker on the shelf.

"A double."

He wasn't ashamed any more. It was the end. He had taken all he could take, right to the end. He hadn't forgotten anything, had he? It was too late to think about that now. Ideas whirled around in his head.

"Another, please."

The bartender here gave him a doubtful look, too.

"Please."

He drank it down in one gulp and threw a hundred-franc note onto the wet counter. He wouldn't need the change.

He had chosen the tree, a big sycamore just on a corner. He only needed to find it again. He had made his landmarks.

If Kitten . . .

Which Kitten? It would have been just the same with another woman. He would have called her Kitten too, or some other nickname, like the chums, and the little ones, and all the others.

Because, when you got right down to it, he was afraid. And now she knew that. They all knew it.

That was his tree, a hundred meters away. He pressed on the accelerator. The Jaguar leaped forward. The trees rushed past him and he felt as if he were absorbing the cars that were coming in the opposite direction.

He had always been afraid.

But not now. Not . . .

He didn't hear the noise, the screeching brakes of the other cars, the footsteps, the voices, the shouts, the shriek of the approaching siren.

It was all over for him.

Epalinges, November 12, 1967